SPARTACUS detail

MEDUSA

The third book of illustrations by
Chris Achilleos

Text by Nigel Suckling

An imprint of Dragon's World Ltd

First published in 1988 by
Dragon's World Ltd
High Street
Limpsfield
Surrey RH8 0DY
Great Britain

© Dragon's World Ltd 1988
© Text Nigel Suckling 1988
© Illustrations Chris Achilleos 1988

No part of this book may be reproduced in any form or by any electronic or mechanical means, including information storage and retrieval systems, without permission in writing from Dragon's World Limited, except by a reviewer who may quote brief passages in a review.

All rights reserved

All illustrations relating to the Jeff Wayne musical of SPARTACUS are the copyright of Spartacus Productions. Their use in any form without prior written permission from Spartacus Productions is strictly forbidden.

Caution: All images are the copyright of Chris Achilleos or the copyright of publishers acknowledged in the text. Their use in any form without prior written permission from Chris Achilleos or the appropriate copyright holder is strictly forbidden.

Designed by Ian Huebner and Chris Achilleos.

British Library Cataloguing in Publication Data
Achilleos, Chris, *1947–*
  Medusa.
  1. English illustrations. Achilleos, Chris, *1947–*.
  Illustrations
  I. Title II. Suckling, Nigel, *1950–*
  741.942

ISBN 1 85028 051 7 Hardcover
ISBN 1 85028 052 5 Paperback

Printed in Singapore

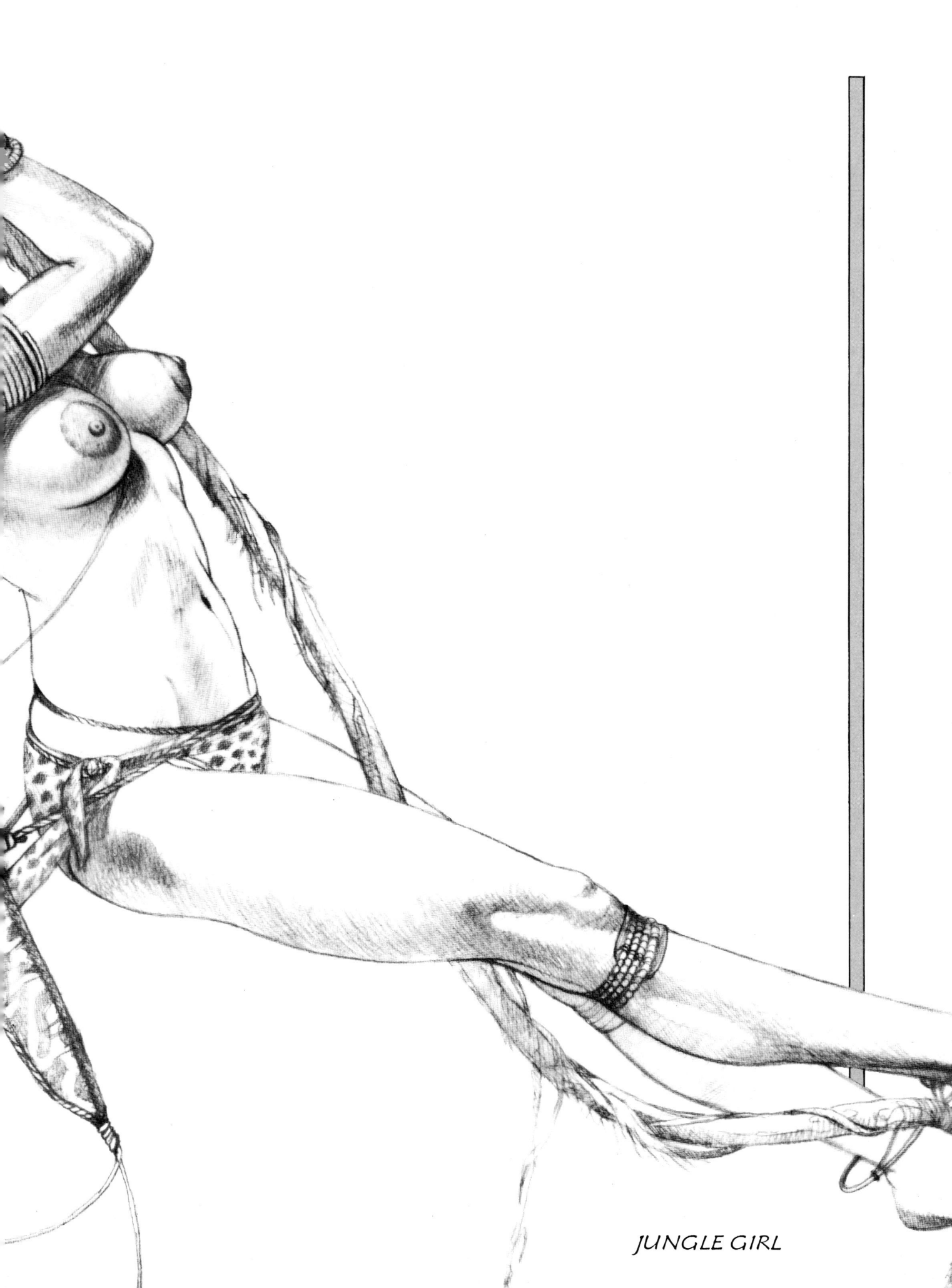

JUNGLE GIRL

CONTENTS

	Foreword	8
	Biography	11
1	Early Work	16
2	Tatoos	20
3	Spartacus	22
4	Painting an Amazon	30
5	Judge Anderson	38
6	Sirens	46
7	Painting an Orc	54
8	Graphic Illustration	62
9	The Heavy Metal Film	66
10	Startrek	76
11	Film Posters	82
12	Amazons	90
13	Supercreeps	106
14	Sky Warriors	118
15	Record Sleeves	128
16	Film and Video	130
17	Pin-Ups	136
	Afterword	142
	Index	143

FOREWORD

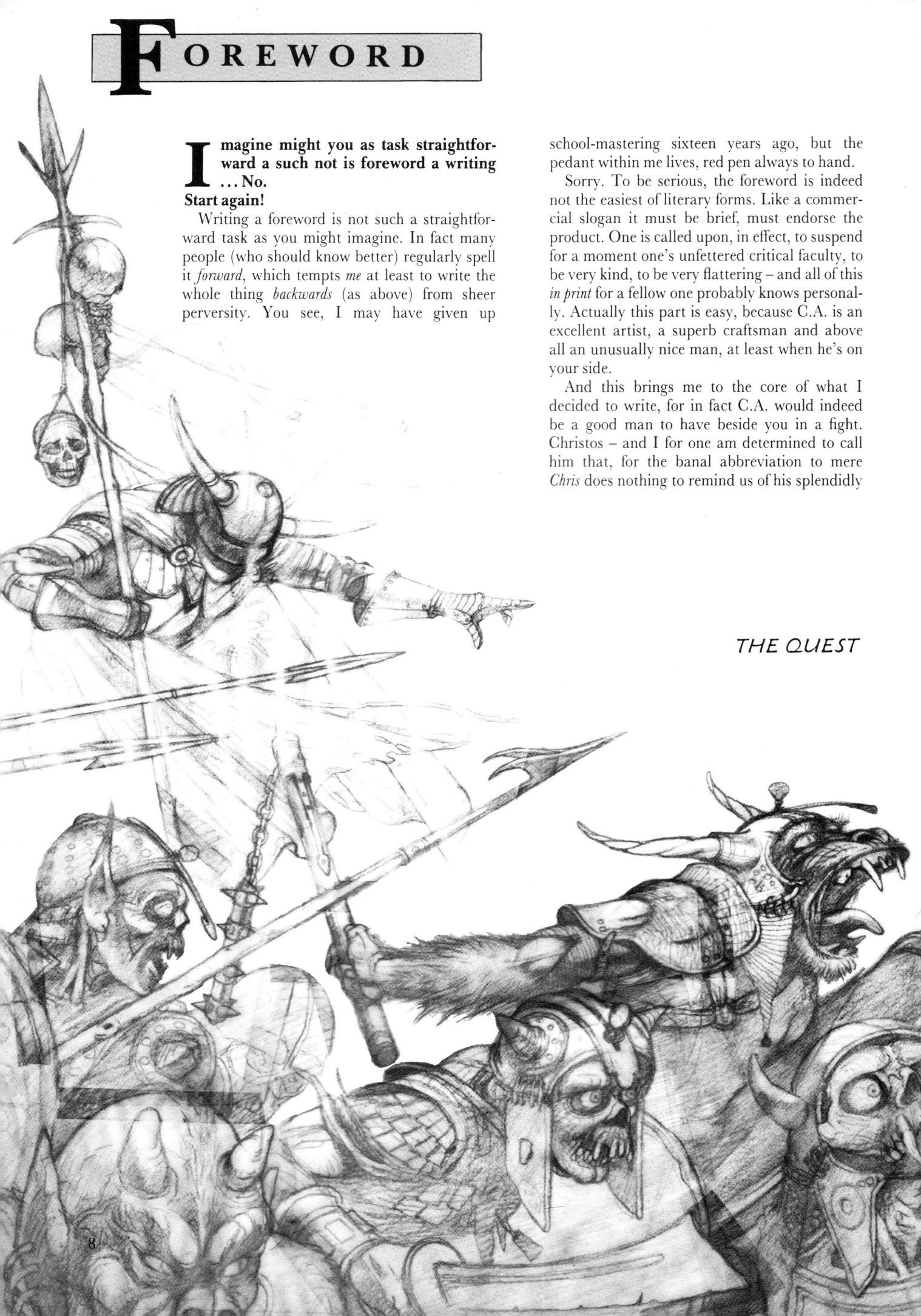

Imagine might you as task straightforward a such not is foreword a writing ... No. **Start again!**

Writing a foreword is not such a straightforward task as you might imagine. In fact many people (who should know better) regularly spell it *forward*, which tempts *me* at least to write the whole thing *backwards* (as above) from sheer perversity. You see, I may have given up school-mastering sixteen years ago, but the pedant within me lives, red pen always to hand.

Sorry. To be serious, the foreword is indeed not the easiest of literary forms. Like a commercial slogan it must be brief, must endorse the product. One is called upon, in effect, to suspend for a moment one's unfettered critical faculty, to be very kind, to be very flattering – and all of this *in print* for a fellow one probably knows personally. Actually this part is easy, because C.A. is an excellent artist, a superb craftsman and above all an unusually nice man, at least when he's on your side.

And this brings me to the core of what I decided to write, for in fact C.A. would indeed be a good man to have beside you in a fight. Christos – and I for one am determined to call him that, for the banal abbreviation to mere *Chris* does nothing to remind us of his splendidly

THE QUEST

Greek origins – Christos is a fighting man. He believes absolutely in the dynamic of conflict, and his art is the only socially acceptable way of putting flesh on his dreams of heroism and danger. So I tend to see him as a marooned soul, the blood-soaked gladiator somehow pitched forward in time by some fatal wound, the war-hero strangely reincarnate in suburban London – even as the great Achilles himself, reduced to jeans and trainers, trading a pencil for his broadsword, a drawing-board for the sun-bleached fields before the mighty walls of ancient Troy.

But what of Helen? Her face it was that launched those thousand ships. A woman it was after all that they were fighting over – or so Homer would have us believe.

And Christos paints women by the bushel, pouting, swaggering, displaying their wares, mutely mouthing the oldest street-vendor's cry

FOREWORD

of them all, but with this addendum: "Well, if you can't afford me, at least don't insult me by not fighting over it!"

Sexuality is fundamental not only in C.A.'s art but also in the dynamic of conflict which I mentioned earlier, and in this way Christos's work, though superficially set in the far future or in the distant past, is totally in tune with this Darwinist age, in which both sex and conflict are widely accepted as positive factors, the mechanics of progress indeed, the facts of life. They displace the related (but how different!) concepts of love and hate, a polarity in which of course only *one* pole can be positive.

But this book is only indirectly about attitudes and ideas. Primarily it is a book about techniques, a fascinating insight into the methods of a superlative craftsman, and as is quite often the case, a sketch may tell us as much as a finely finished painting, a description of the methods of production may be as interesting as the product itself. In this book we are privileged to admire not only Christos's preliminary drawings – so dynamic, so immediate – but also the painting process itself. The image takes shape *before our very eyes*.

And so the dream is made flesh (almost) by art, and suddenly we can actually peer into another man's head. Miraculous, were it not today so commonplace. For the artist is the magic man, the maker of mysteries. He holds the keys to another world.

And art is the polished shield of Perseus. While revealing a reality far too dangerous to be confronted directly, it nonetheless enables us, through vision, to destroy what might destroy us – Medusa herself.

Patrick Woodroffe
April 1988

BIOGRAPHY

For those unlucky enough not to possess a copy of *Sirens* yet, here is a brief sketch of Chris Achilleos' life and career so far.

He was born in Cyprus into a Greek-Cypriot family that moved to London, England, when he was twelve years old. The sudden transfer to a completely alien culture and climate was fairly traumatic, but ultimately it played a possibly decisive part in his choice of career. Faced with having to master a completely new alphabet and language, Chris tended to concentrate his energies in school on art and craft subjects, where they hardly mattered. His imagination was also stimulated by the wealth of visual entertainment suddenly at his fingertips, particularly comics, which provided one of his first artistic heroes, Frank Bellamy of the *Eagle*.

From school he attended Hornsey College of Art, specialising in scientific and technical illustration, which may sound rather uninspiring but it did teach the basic techniques of illustration, which have served him well ever since, in particular the use of the airbrush, which was soon to become enormously popular through the work of such innovators as Alan Aldridge and Michael English. The college was also generous in allowing him time to develop his own interests.

After graduating with honours, Chris struggled for a while as a technical illustrator before chasing an old ambition of illustrating book covers. Enquiries led him to the Brian Boyle studios, who commissioned a short series of covers on the strength of his portfolio, thus initiating the prolific chain of cover illustrations that forms the backbone of his work to date.

They are far from being his only line, however. Examples of others may be found in the two Achilleos collections published so far by Paper Tiger – *Beauty and the Beast* (1978) and *Sirens* (1986) – plus of course this volume, where we will be examining his techniques in more detail.

Chris Achilleos lives beside Epping Forest in north-east London and has two daughters. His marriage ended soon after the publication of *Sirens*.

A separate drawing concentrating on the head of the Dragon.

The first small rough concept drawing. I quickly dropped this because I felt that the Dragon looked lifeless and without soul.

This is the main pencil working drawing shown here the same size as the original. I later decided that the Dragon's head was too large and so re-drew it a little smaller.

DRAGONSPELL

1 EARLY WORK

The marginal drawings on this page are taken from Chris's unofficial college sketchbooks into which he poured his true spirit whenever he could. In hindsight it is not at all surprising he did not long remain a technical illustrator, though the way out was far from clear at the time.

The two central pictures are earlier, dating from his schooldays. They were executed with pencil and ballpoint pen on lining wallpaper, which was all he could find large enough to match his ambitions. Unfortunately no one warned him that the paper would soon discolour and fall apart. The galley picture has in fact completely disintegrated into long strips now, intimations of which are visible in the reproduction, and the other is not far behind. One can also see on the galley sail a faint pencilled eagle design which was originally much bolder.

Both pictures were based on scenes in the *Eagle* comic strip, *Heroes of Sparta*, which was usually though not always illustrated by Frank Bellamy.

The approach used was to expand the tiny original to an epic scale, exaggerating the proportions and emphasis of the composition where necessary for increased dramatic effect, and then add a wealth of detail and shading for which there was previously no room.

In the shading with pencil and ballpoint Chris says he learned the airbrush principle of achieving depth and roundness with graduated tones without ever having heard of the airbrush. At least part of the subtlety achieved is due to the time spent choosing his ballpoints, making sure they did not smudge when changing direction, a habit which did not endear him to shop assistants!

On page 18 are some more examples from his unofficial college sketchbook. Their extreme violence is probably half due to the extremely boring nature of whatever exercise he was really supposed to be doing at the time.

Partly also it comes from Robert E. Howard's *Conan* books, which he was then devouring avidly. Looking back, he cannot remember questioning the violence much, seeing it only as excitement, and believes this to be common among youths on the threshold of manhood. Being fresh to physical maturity, their main fantasies are about its exercise, i.e. sex and violence. Considerations of subtlety and prudence come later.

On page 19 is a black and white self-promotion poster Chris produced for an agency he joined after leaving the Brian Boyle studio, done when he had no inkling that he would one day be famous for his pin-ups and Amazons. In her left hand the girl is holding no ray-gun but an airbrush.

Surrounding it are examples of the standard airbrush exercises required of Hornsey's technical illustration class. Though they were very tedious, Chris believes they were essential for a proper grasp of technique. He is occasionally astonished by young enthusiasts who think they can just 'pick up an airbrush and wave it like a magic wand to achieve instant success'.

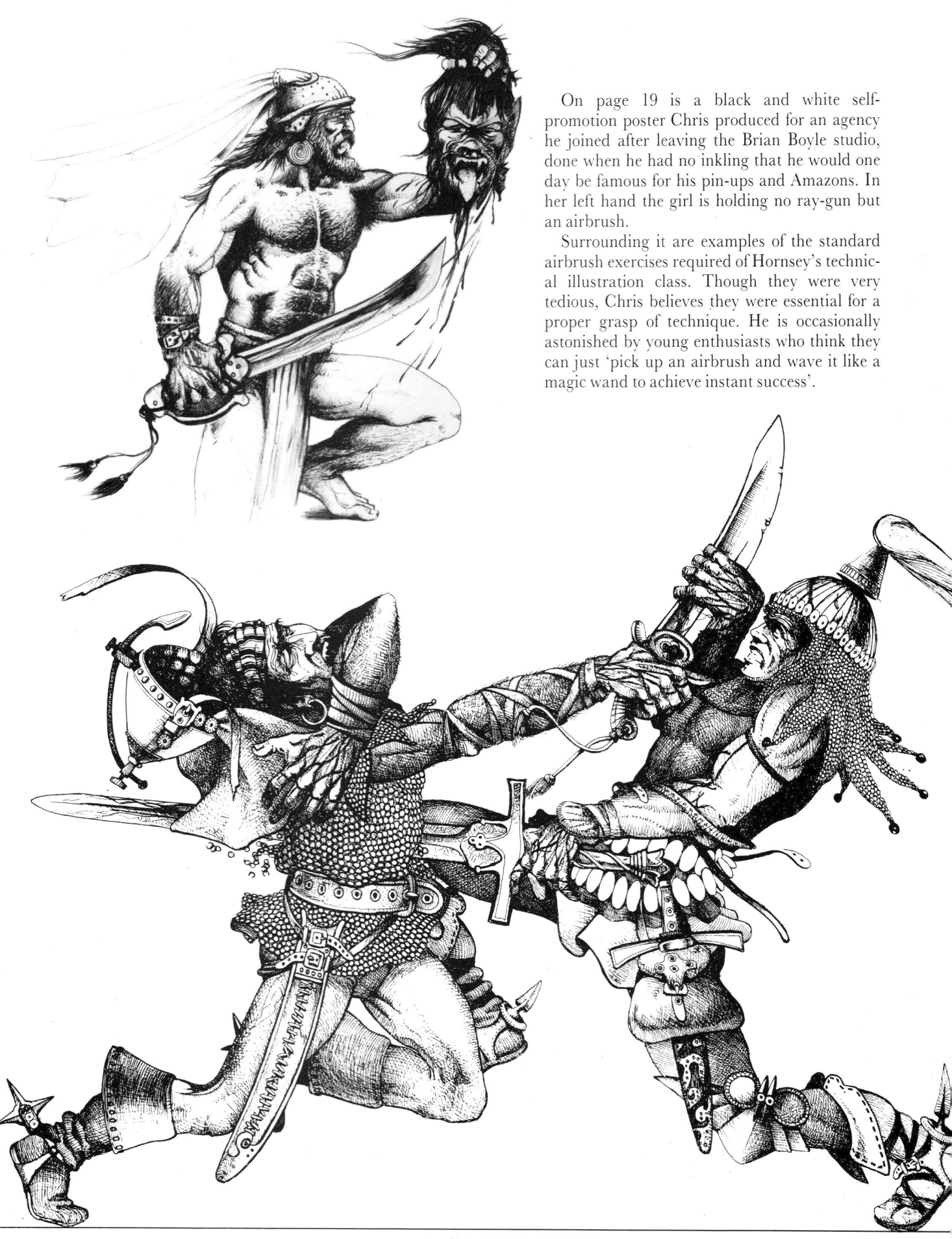

Most of the exercises were aimed at achieving 3-D effects and differing surface textures (some of which are more obviously relevant to Chris's later work than others!). Those at the foot of the page were freehand attempts to draw straight lines while simultaneously tapering off the ink flow, which is not at all easy.

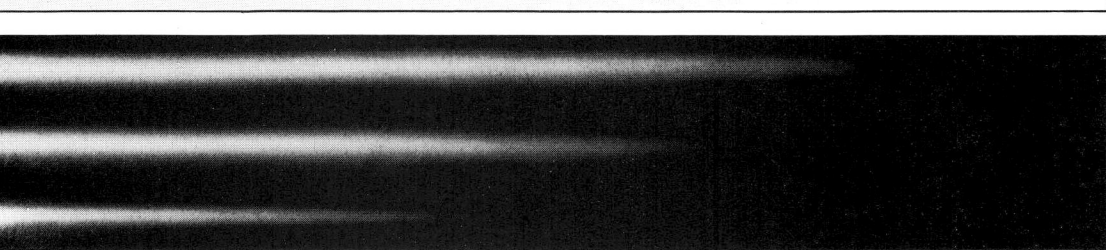

2 TATTOOS

Chris Achilleos' direct involvement with the field of tattooing stems from an encounter with Chris Wroblewski, a photographer specialising in tattoos, at the Frankfurt Book Fair.

There he learned of the immense popularity of snatched bits of Achilleos designs in tattoo parlours. This did not come as a complete surprise since he had noticed his work adorning other people's flesh in the streets and on television, but he had no idea of the true extent of his influence.

In 1987 Chris attended a tattooing conference and found his pictures everywhere. In one demonstration a fan was even having a fair copy of the complete *Heavy Metal* film poster tattooed right across his back.

To begin with Chris wandered round the conference anonymously, but later he was introduced by Lal Hardy, a famed tattooist from North London, to some of the participants and was made to feel like some kind of superstar. Among his greatest admirers are Dutch, German and Austrian tattooists.

Not content with having his designs adapted (not to mention nicked) by tattooists, Chris has lately turned his hand to producing some directly for the medium, examples of which are shown here with his own comments. There is talk of producing a limited edition of Achilleos designs for tattoo parlours, but this is still tentative.

A

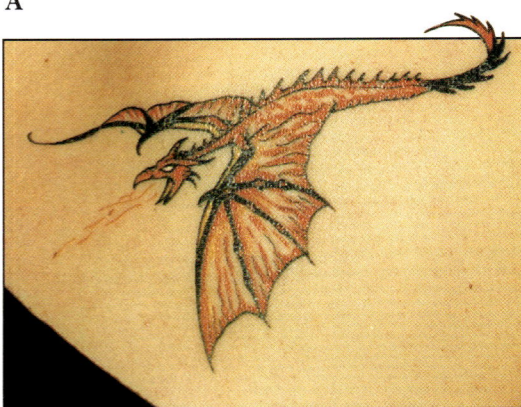

B

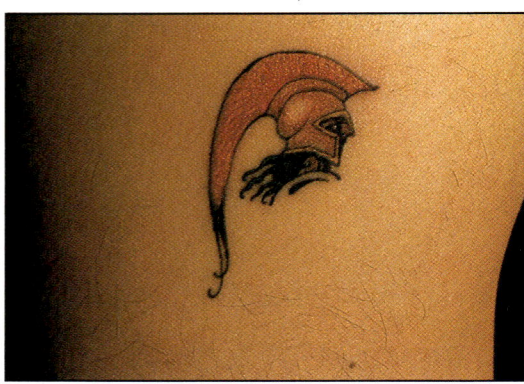

C

A This shows a design cleverly adapted from my cover for a Whitesnake album by Filip Lev of Switzerland. Clients often go to tattoo parlours with books, record covers or ideas of their own to copy. The original of the design can be seen on page 129.

B This is my own design done specially for a friend, Tracie. It was tattooed by Lal Hardy, who also did the following ones.

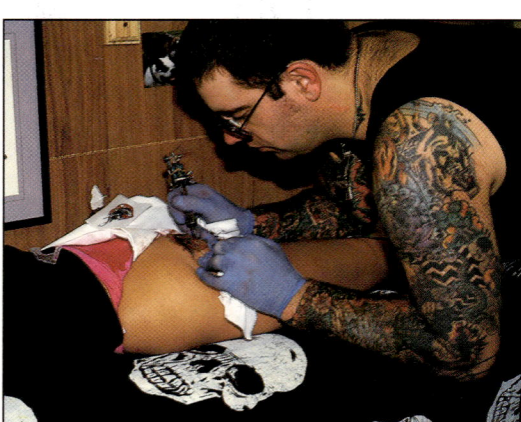

D

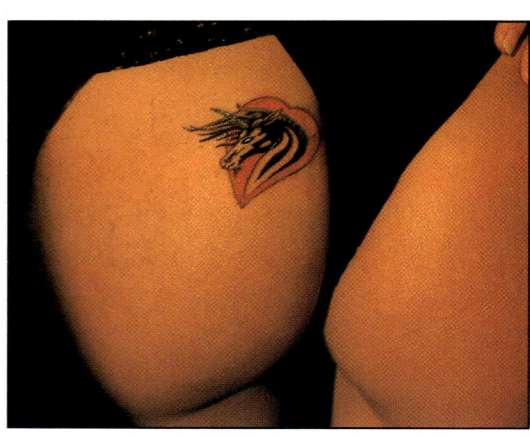

E

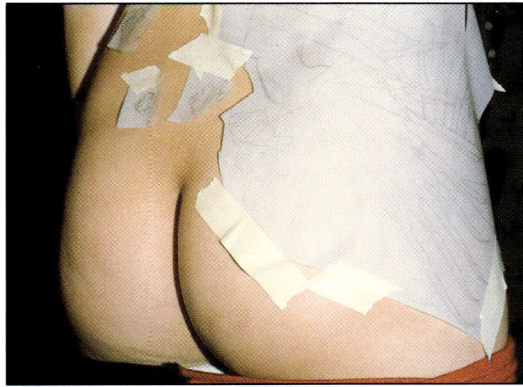

F

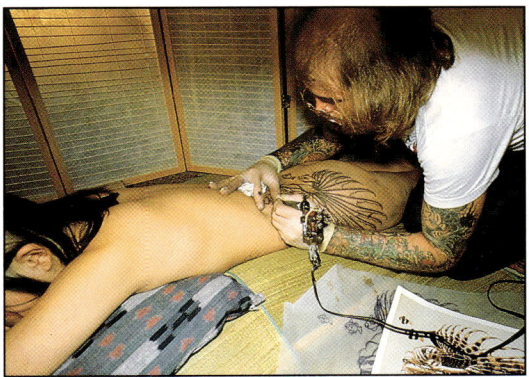

G

H

C I had this done for myself.

D My girlfriend's choice was a unicorn, so I designed this for her. Here we see Lal applying it.

E And here is the finished product. Because Michelle is a model the tattoo had to be somewhere inconspicuous.

F To match my design to the girl's figure I drew it on tracing paper, which was then wrapped around her so that I could change the proportions of the original drawing as necessary.

G A kind of carbon paper was used to trace a guide to the drawing onto Yuki's skin. Here Ian is drawing in the outline with the tracing paper and a reproduction of the original painting for reference.

H This shows the completed outline of my design before colouring begins.

The pictures F–H are also featured in Chris Wroblewski's forthcoming book on tattoos, provisionally titled *Skin Show II*, in which the process will be analysed more closely. The tattooing was carried out by Ian of Reading (his professional title) over some two hours and was closely monitored by both still and movie cameras. The basis of the design was the mermaid that appears in *Beauty and the Beast*, which was chosen by the Japanese girl, Yuki.

Chris has some misgivings about tattoos because, he says, there are so many bad and tasteless examples around, mostly on young people who don't know any better. He believes tattoos are acceptable only if they enhance or at least liven up a body. For example, if Yuki had wanted a monster planted right across her chest he would have had nothing to do with it, but as it is he is quite happy.

Acknowledgements:
Mermaid tattoo by Ian of Reading
Studio setting courtesy of Neal St East, London
Colour by Lancaster Laboratory, London
Photos by Chris Wroblewski/Tim Coleman
Book to be published by Virgin Books: *Skin Show II*

3 SPARTACUS

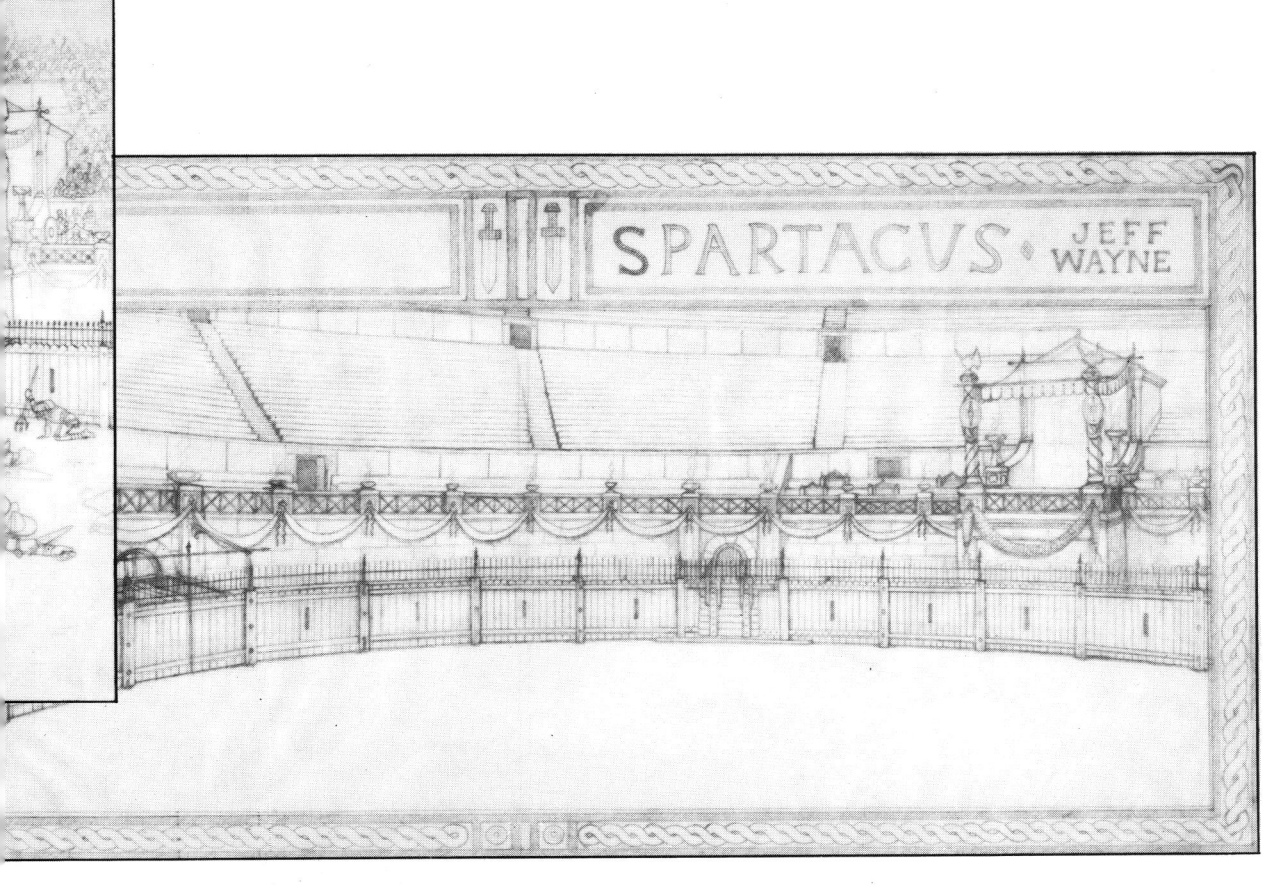

WAYNE'S MUSICAL VERSION OF SPARTACUS

Chris Achilleos was originally contacted in about 1983 by John Pasche, then art director of this project, and asked if he was interested in submitting some speculative designs for a proposed musical version of *Spartacus* by Jeff Wayne (famous among other things for his enormously successful musical adaptation of H. G. Wells's *War of the Worlds*). Chris naturally was and, in competition with other artists, sent along several rough designs, which won him the commission. Two of them are shown above.

From this promising start the assignment somehow drifted into limbo until about two years later, when Pasche rang again to see if he was still interested. By now Achilleos was much less so, but was won back by a personal meeting with Jeff Wayne.

The package comprised four large and very detailed paintings with equally detailed borders executed in Roman style as frescos, mosaics or bas-reliefs. Also a map and some small drawings to decorate the lyric-sheets. An essential requirement was that the pictures should not only be exciting but historically accurate, since the tale is a true and well-documented one.

On the previous page the top picture is a visual synopsis of the drama showing the two main protagonists against a fresco of the forces they represent – Spartacus the Thracian with his unruly horde of escaped gladiators and slaves with a variety of pillaged arms, and Marcus Crassus with his orderly regiments of a Rome shaken almost to its foundations by the revolt.

In case one is tempted to side with the forces of order too easily, the scene below shows the dark side of Rome, the barbaric popular entertainments that were an everyday feature of Roman life and which sparked the uprising. Chris sees a parallel between them and today's television and video nasties.

In Rome the authorities cultivated the games largely to keep the masses happy, to help them ignore the barbarians trying to invade the empire and the corrupt politicians who ruled them. The games were conducted according to very strict and formalised rules, each pair of gladiators having a referee who marked out an area within which they must keep.

In the quest for accuracy and relevance to the musical script, each stage of these pictures was minutely thrashed out with the others involved in the project – an often frustrating but ultimately rewarding process.

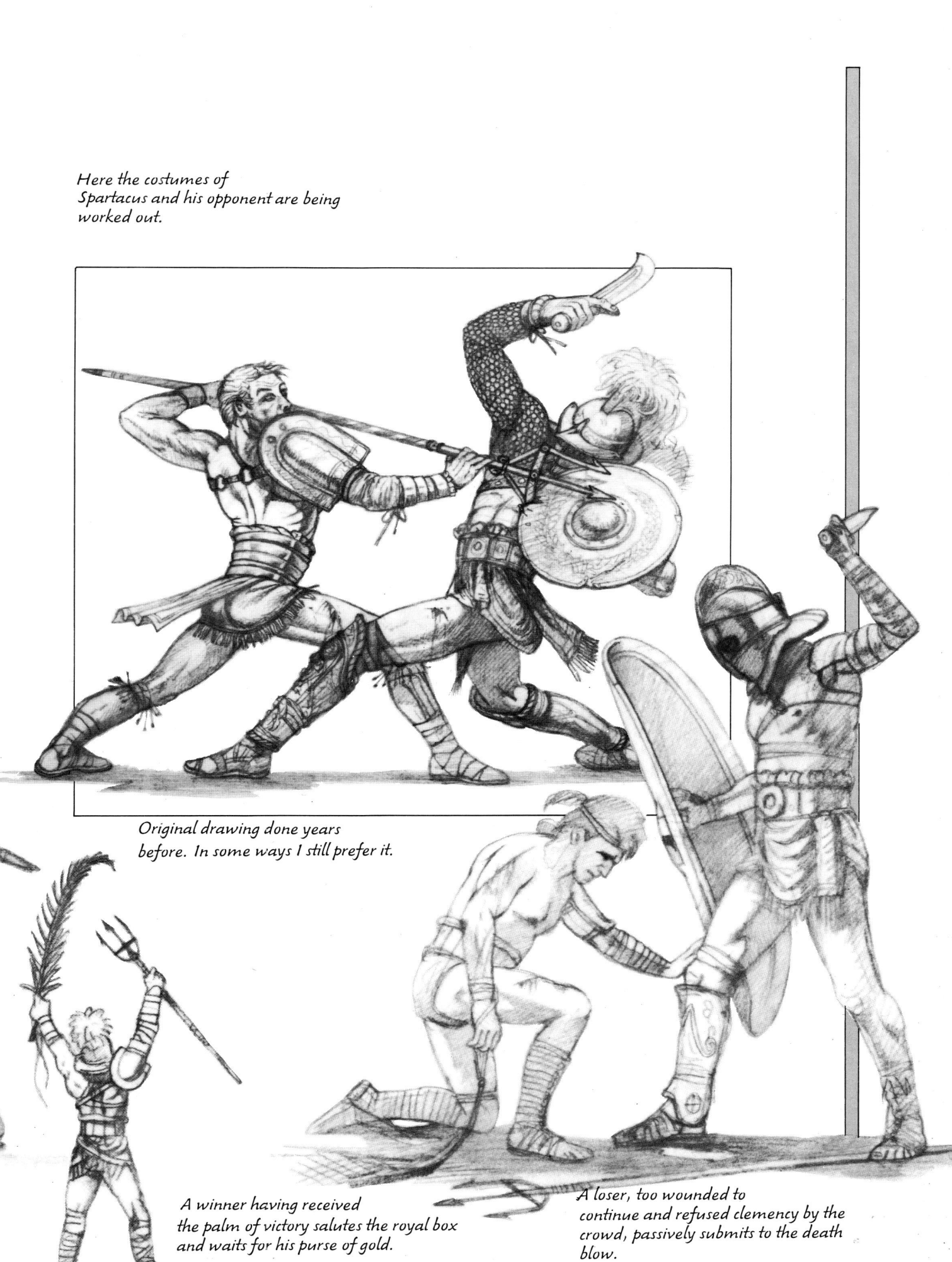

The sketch below was not used in the end. It shows the gladiators escaping from their barracks, arming themselves in the kitchens and attacking Roman guards to gain more arms. This pattern repeated led to them finally equipping an army of 90,000 freed slaves.

The border above shows the rebels escaping down Mt Vesuvius on ropes made from wild vines. They had been trapped there by a Roman force, which rashly decided to wait until morning for their attack.

4 PAINTING AN AMAZON

Achilleos' famous pictures of Amazons have appeared in many different formats. For those who wish to paint one of their own, here is a step-by-step exposé of how he goes about it.

This picture was commissioned by Paper Tiger for the cover of their *Heroic Dreams* book. As with any commission the first thing, before setting pencil to paper, was to define the limits of the job.

In this case time was an important factor; it had to be produced quickly, so a simple, bold design was called for. The cover lettering had also already been decided, so this fixed the framework of any illustration – in this case a large square in the lower part of the page. Then came the general nature of the picture and the suggestion of an Amazon was acceptable to the publishers.

A standing figure was first considered, but Chris felt it would be a waste of space, since it would be too small to effectively grab the passing eye from a bookshelf – essential for a cover. Thus came about the kneeling figure in the first rough, A.

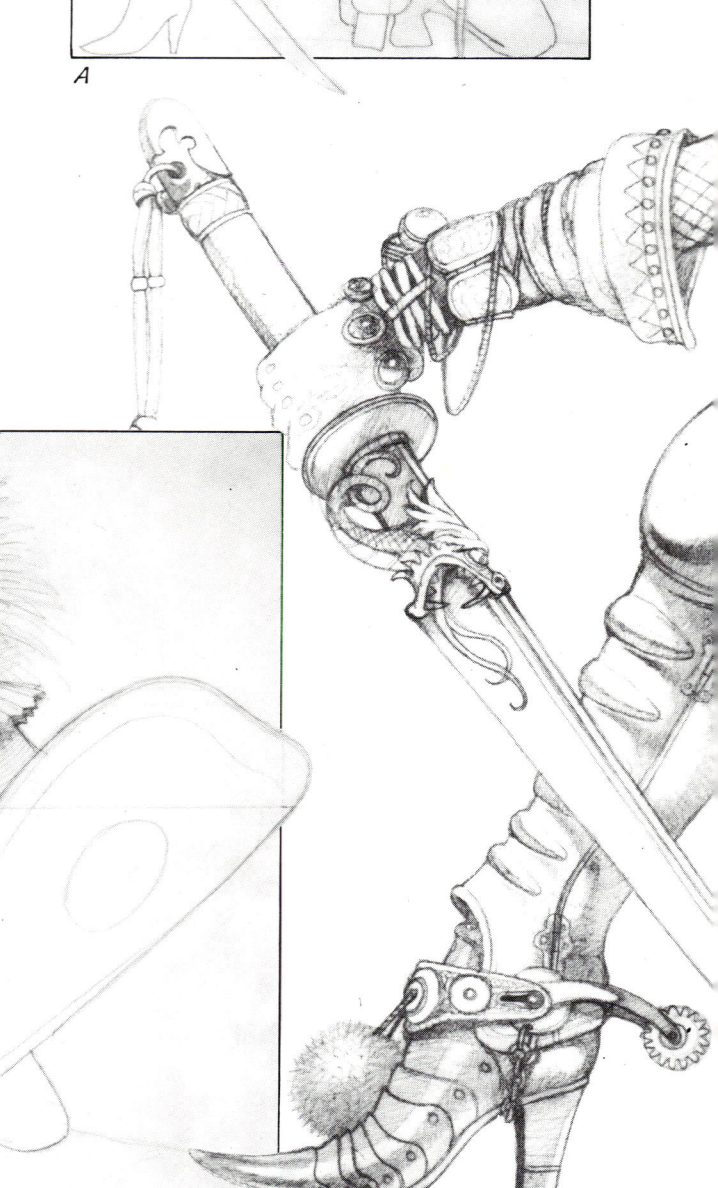

A

The second drawing done on a separate sheet of tracing paper, placed on top of the first and taken further by adding the shield, boots, etc.

This is the enlarged and final drawing w everything is finalised and later transferr the artboard.

As usual, the head is drawn separately and placed on top of the figure to view.

On reflection, the first rough did not seem quite dynamic enough, so a long shield was introduced (p.30, B) to make a dramatic V with the sword and echo the angle of the raised leg. This rough was shown to the publishers and accepted.

The shield and costume were then further refined in stages to produce the first working drawing (p.31, C), in which the head is left vague to be worked on separately.

A detail to note is the embellishment on the sword-blade. Although pleased with it in some ways Chris was uneasy, partly from a design point of view and partly because he detests baroque weaponry.

The shield was another dilemma. Its slightly asymmetrical outline seemed right, but its patterning was a problem. Decisions on both points were postponed to later stages.

The head above is the same size as the original.

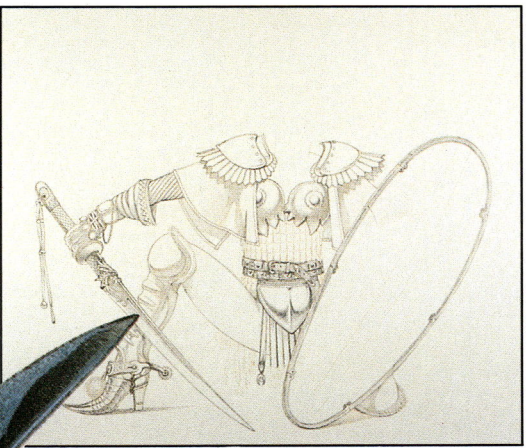

A The image having been transferred to board, it is pencilled over. Head still undecided.

B The decided elements are inked in and the head superimposed. A faint circle shows the likely extent of the finished headdress.

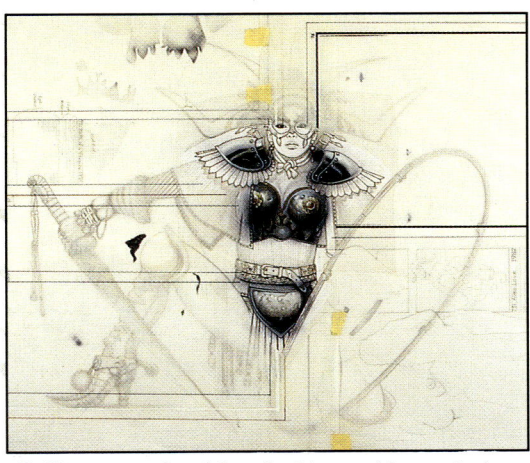

C The area to be airbrushed is roughly masked with old bits of tracing paper, then exactly masked with Frisk film cut round the outline.

D Armour is painted in and undercolour laid down for scales on stomach and shoulders. Masking removed for inspection.

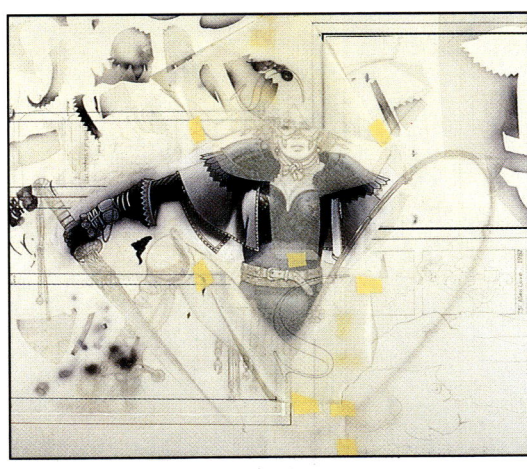

E Masking returned and Frisk film cut out round arm and scaled mantle on shoulders.

F Further inspection to gauge progress. Sword-blade and shield patterning still undecided.

G From here on the masking goes on and off between each stage. A decision is made on the sword-blade.

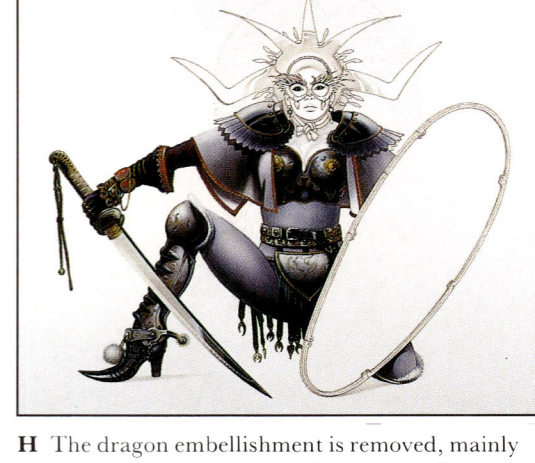

H The dragon embellishment is removed, mainly because it distracts the attention from the face area, which is to be the main focus.

I The shield rim of Celtic design is painted in, slightly reducing the area of uncertainty.

J Preparations are made for tackling the face, introducing the first real splash of colour.

K Flesh undercoats are sprayed in by airbrush. Toning is done by hand with small sable brushes.

L With masked airbrushing you can only see the area being worked on. For undertones this is all right, but for the final balance all masking comes off.

M More detail put in by hand on mouth and cleavage. Scales hand-painted over undercoat. Only shield and headdress remain uncertain.

N Original drawing superimposed on painting. Shield boss simplified and decision made to go for bright colours.

O Having done shield I instantly realised it was far too powerful, again distracting attention from face area.

P I attempted to quieten shield by blacking out yellow areas, but it was still not enough.

Q A black acetate overlay covering complete shield pattern is tested for effect, which finally works.

R Shield painted over and rough overlay of headdress tried out and approved. Note masking tape holding the acetate.

Here we have the finished product one and a half times its size on the *Heroic Dreams* cover. Within the basic bold geometric structure it can be seen that there has been room for many subtle details which draw the eye here and there while always returning it to the main area of focus.

It is also worth noting how the basically masculine severity of the Amazon's costume has been softened by careful contrasts – in the headdress, for instance, or the boot, whose aggressive spike is offset by the pompon dangling from the spur. Similarly the sword's vicious sweep is balanced by the tassel on its hilt.

No detail is as accidental as it may seem. For instance, the gold chain looped around the girl's wrist was introduced to strengthen the narrow wrist and soften the right angle between arm and sword.

In the stage-by-stage comments we dealt mainly with the painting; perhaps more needs to be said about the designing.

First the drawing. Once Chris has a vague picture in his mind of what is required, he does a thumbnail sketch on tracing paper, which has several advantages over the opaque kind. For a start it is possible to work on both sides, changing elements of the design without committing yourself too much each time. Also, defects often show up when a drawing is reversed.

When a working drawing has been achieved it is transferred to illustration board by means of red or grey carbon-like paper, the outlines being traced with a 7H pencil. The transferred image is then worked over and brought to life with a softer pencil, which varies with the type of board, along with any improvements that spring to mind. This means that before painting begins the picture has been drawn at least three times. It is a laborious process, but Chris finds it essential for getting close to perfection with these materials.

The medium used for this and all his recent work is mostly Chromacolour cell paint, normally used by film animators. It is vivid, non-fading and may either be diluted for airbrushing or painted on neat.

The board is stippled watercolour board, which allows more freedom for texturing than the usual hard airbrush board.

HEROIC DREAM

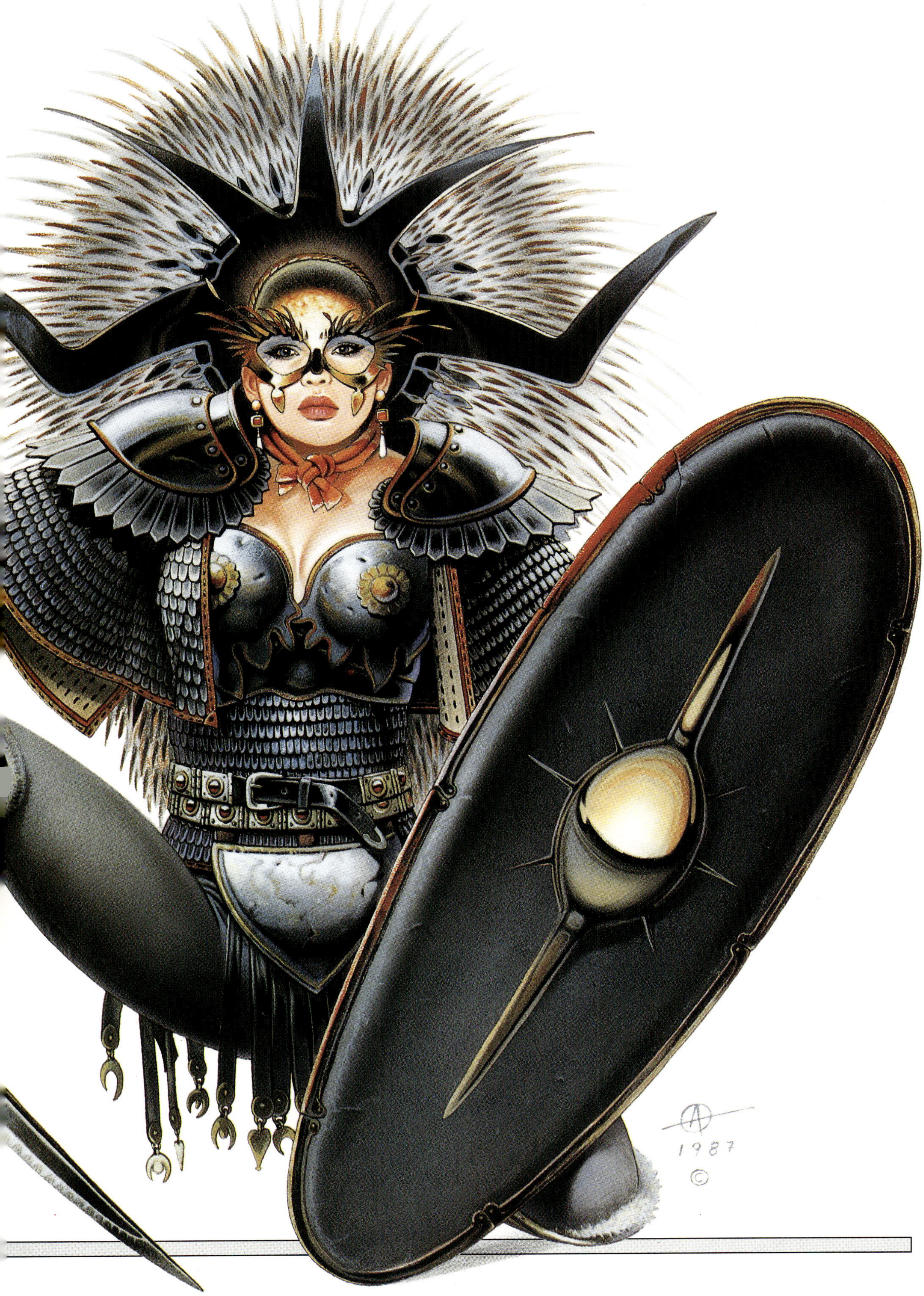
1987 ©

5 JUDGE ANDERSON

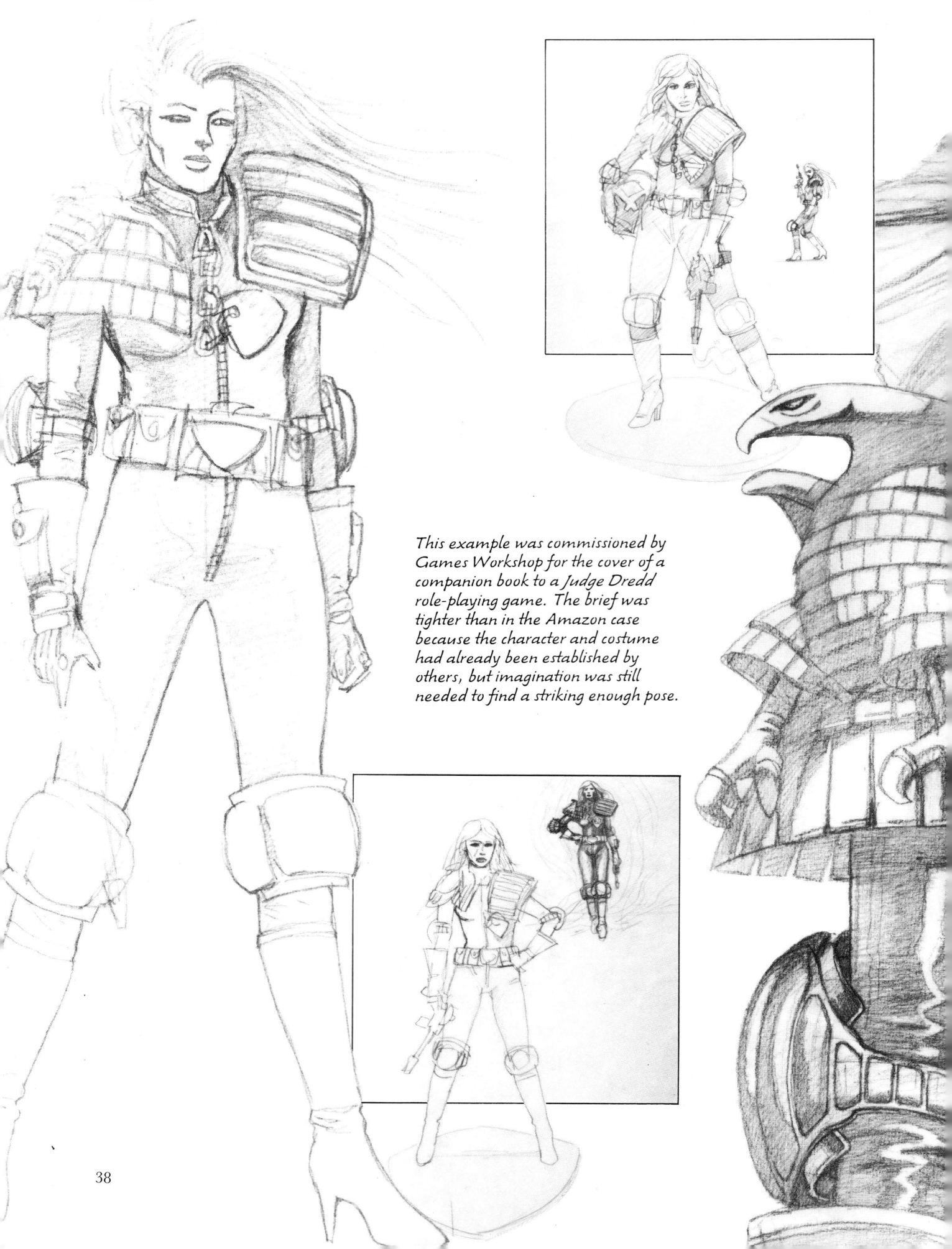

This example was commissioned by Games Workshop for the cover of a companion book to a Judge Dredd role-playing game. The brief was tighter than in the Amazon case because the character and costume had already been established by others, but imagination was still needed to find a striking enough pose.

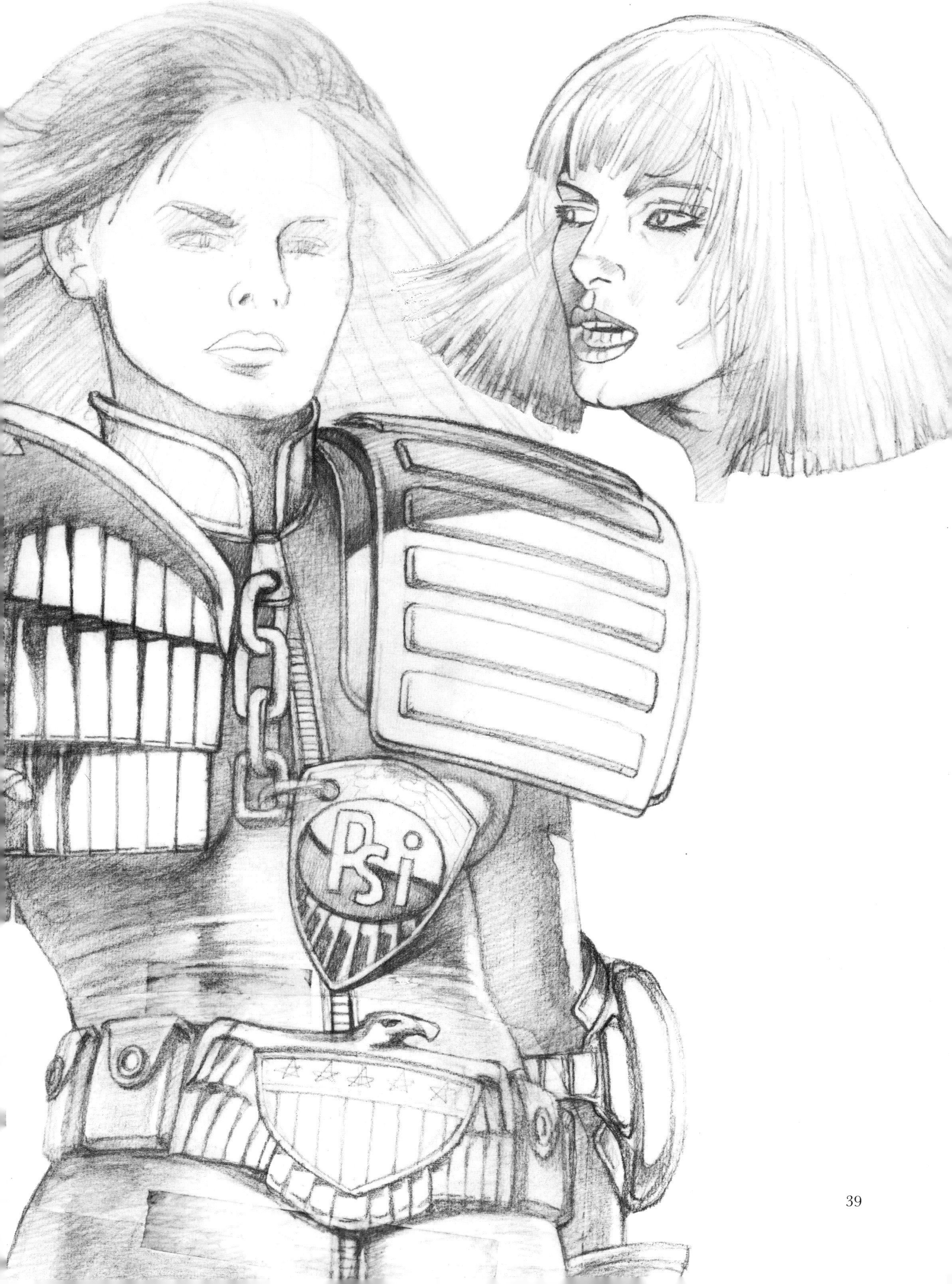
Psi

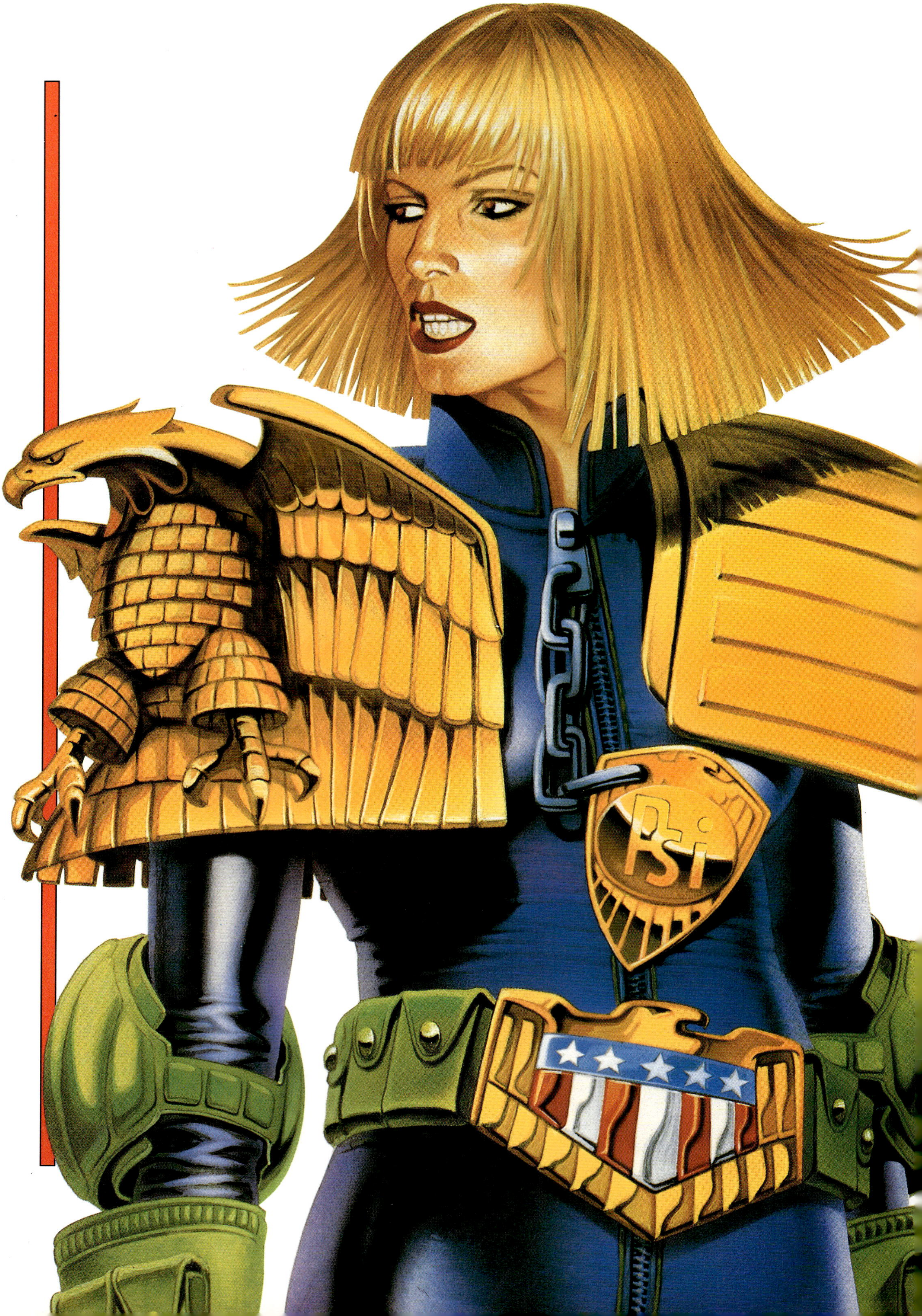
PSI

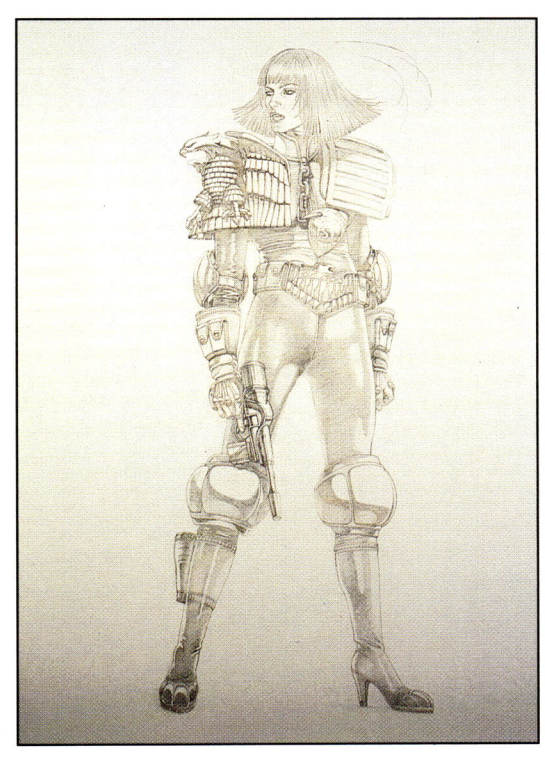

A The working drawing is transferred to board and shaded with pencil. Outlines are not inked in as usual because of synthetic effect being aimed at.

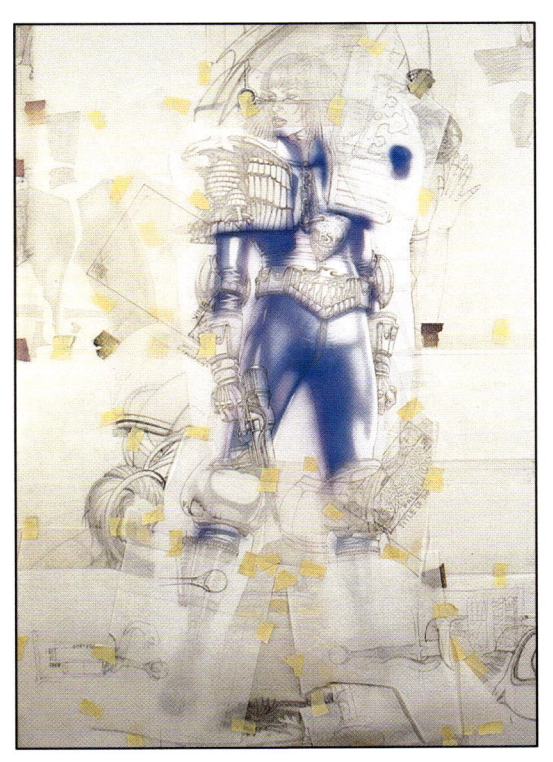

B Largest area of colour tackled first with airbrush, being built up in very thin layers. Highlights achieved by scraping and rubbing out

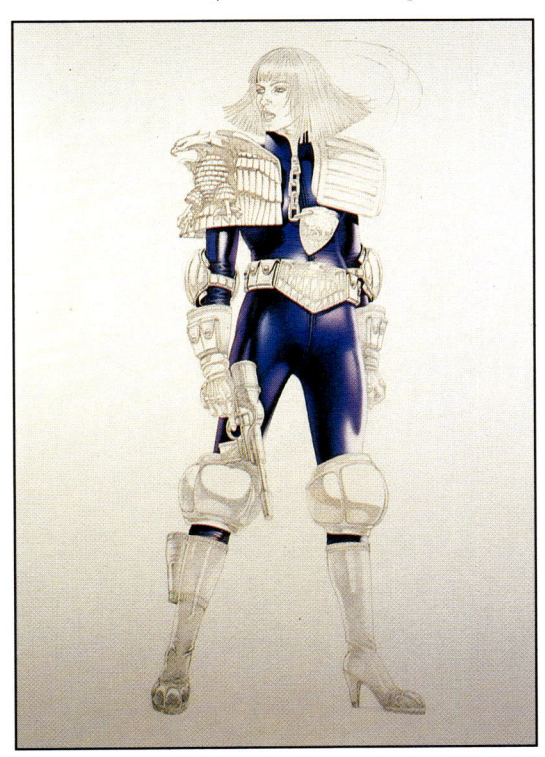

C Masking removed for inspection. Note comic-type movement lines behind head, later dropped.

D Green area tackled and colour balance checked. This needed care because of tricky contrast, which could easily look garish.

41

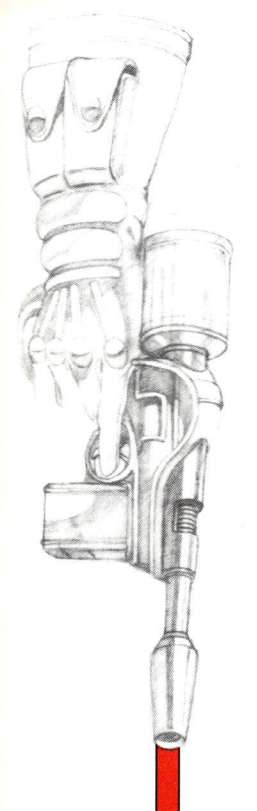

E Badge and waist buckle completed and whole picture viewed.

F Further work done on shoulder guards. Note shadow of hair.

G On reflection I decided the blue was not dark enough, so here the area is masked off again and gone over with blue-black paint.

H Painting completely masked out save for head. First Chroma Colour mixed in ceramic pots.

I Frisk film laid down and cut out around hair, face and neck. Hair area removed and colour built up in tones of yellow and orange.

J Masking of face and neck removed, hair masking returned to protect it during work on face and neck.

K Face gradually built up in tones of colour.

L Colour strengthening done by hand on lips, nose and eyes. No opaque colour used so far.

M Colours made opaque by mixing with white. White also used neat as highlights. Hair masking removed for very fine retouching around edges.

N All masking removed for final inspection and nit-picking. Sometimes this can take all day because no painting is ever really finished.

The basic requirement of this commission was for a standing pose. After various trials the one on page 39 seemed about right, but it still lacked something. To inject more life into it Chris used a trick he often employs in cases where he is not required to illustrate a particular incident; he imagined a scenario of his own.

In the game and the comic-strip it derives from Anderson is a Psi-judge, a kind of psychic policewoman. In the world of AD 2000 she has more of a sense of humour than the other Mega-city judges, but is a tough cookie none the less. In his scenario Chris imagined her walking down a street past a gang of roadworkers, one of whom ogles her in time-honoured fashion, thinking something like: 'What a neat ass!'

Being psychic she naturally senses it and swings round demanding: 'What creep thought that?'

A similar trick was used for the illustration on pages 14–15. There the publisher's brief simply called for a dragon in a fantasy setting, and all the details arose from a story Chris dreamed up in which the dragon is in fact a shape-shifting wizard come to attack a rival's stronghold. Having destroyed the causeway leading to the castle gate along with the flower of the resident chivalry, the dragon now faces the rival sorcerer himself and for just a moment is entranced by the mystic light he wields. What happens next is left to our imaginations.

When illustrating an established character like Judge Anderson careful research is necessary, which is as much a hallmark of Chris's work as his rampant imagination when given more freedom.

He already knew the character from the *Dredd* comics, which provided most of the details needed to go ahead, but there had occasionally been small changes in the costume. To check the latest state of play he rang Judge Anderson's creator.

Something Chris was not too happy about was the colour of the leggings and arm guards. To his mind it is dreadful and should rather have been red, but since it had already been established he had to make the best of it.

The paint used was Chroma Colour cell paint. The board was Oram & Robertson hard line board, which was worked almost entirely by airbrush because from the outset Chris wanted Anderson to look almost robotic, with only a slight rubbery texture to her costume and a hard plastic or metallic look to the accessories. He tackled the job almost entirely as if it were a technical illustration, 'as if she were a spark plug'.

JUDGE ANDERSON

45

6 PAINTING SIRENS

This is my main working drawing for The Sirens' Remorse. The second siren was introduced at a late stage to balance the composition. The picture actually faced the other way to begin with, but in the end looked better like this.

From the beginning I did not want my siren to have the usual scaly mermaid's tail. I have always felt that if mermaids truly existed they would, being mammals, have smooth tails like seals.

47

THE SIRENS' REMORSE detail

A The working drawing is transferred to board, pencilled in and outlined with sepia ink.

B The sea is tackled first, everything else being masked off with Frisk film. Colour is applied with airbrush and freehand painting.

C More detailed work done on water in the foreground, the masking being left in place.

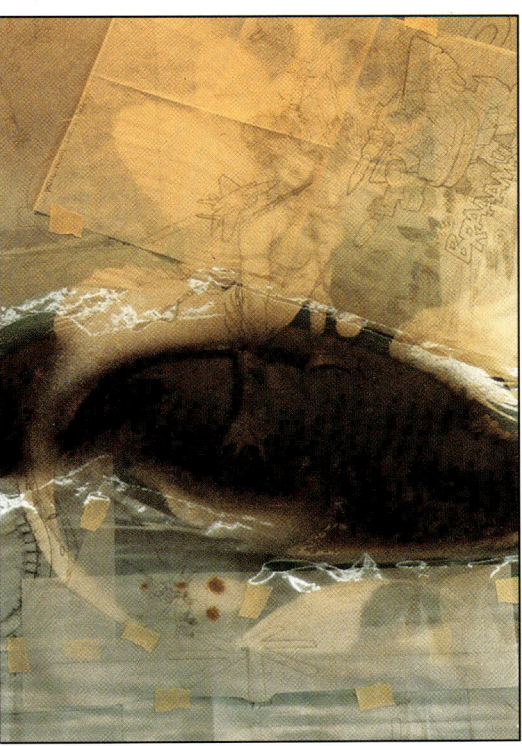

D Next to be tackled is the rock. Outlines of old drawings can be seen in the rough mask.

E Masking removed for inspection and detailed hand-work done on crab and hundreds of limpets.

F Starting with second siren, the eyes are outlined in sepia. Note how photo references can be used to enhance realism.

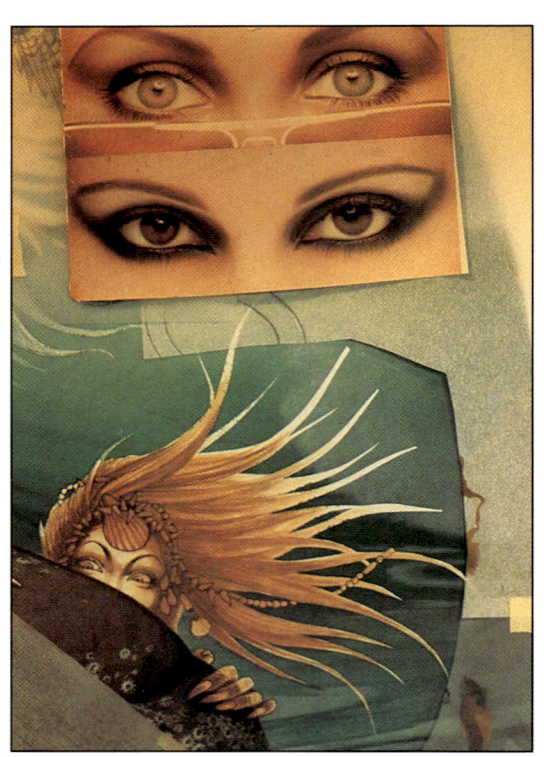

G Hair painted in manually. Face is underpainted in tones of sepia, yellow and orange.

H Opaque colour introduced for flesh tones. Hair strands picked out in white against the waves.

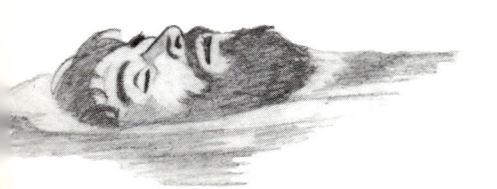

I Now the main work begins. The siren's body is airbrushed with sepia and orange tones, then surface painted freehand.

J Masking removed to check progress and attention given to breast area.

K More detail work done on body, particularly the scaly arm and claws. Camouflage pattern for tail decided on.

L Tail patterned, leaving only hair and minor details to finish off on siren. Drowned sailor is last to receive attention.

This picture was commissioned for the cover of *Sirens*, the second compilation of Chris Achilleos' work. It is a rare example of him being given a completely free hand with a subject. It was also the first picture he painted almost entirely with Chroma Colour cell paint, instead of his previous mixed media, a practice he intends to continue. The board was Oram & Robertson watercolour board.

THE SIRENS' REMORSE

7 PAINTING AN ORC

Small preparatory sketch.

Sketch blown up to working size for further development.

55

paintings. Usually any further wrinkles are removed as the paper dries, but here Chris found that cell paint tends to set like glue. This was not disastrous, but he has no plans to repeat the experiment.

THE ORC'S WAR BANNER detail

For this picture Chris further experimented with Chroma Colour on stretched rag-paper, a surface he has often used with other paints and dyes.

The first step is to soak a sheet of coloured paper in a shower and tape it firmly to a drawing board. As it dries it stretches, losing its wrinkles and presenting a beautiful surface for 'action'

THE ORC'S WAR BANNER

This commission was for the cover of a new book by Ian Livingstone. As often happens with Fighting Fantasy, Chris worked under two different pressures – Livingstone wanting it as gory as possible and the publishers wanting the violence toned down. One feels the publishers lost out in the end, though they did succeed in having an arrow removed from the foreground victim's throat.

Otherwise the brief was very loose and Chris imagined his own tale to account for the scene. Usually this is a pleasure, but occasionally, he says, too much freedom in a brief can be as trying as too little.

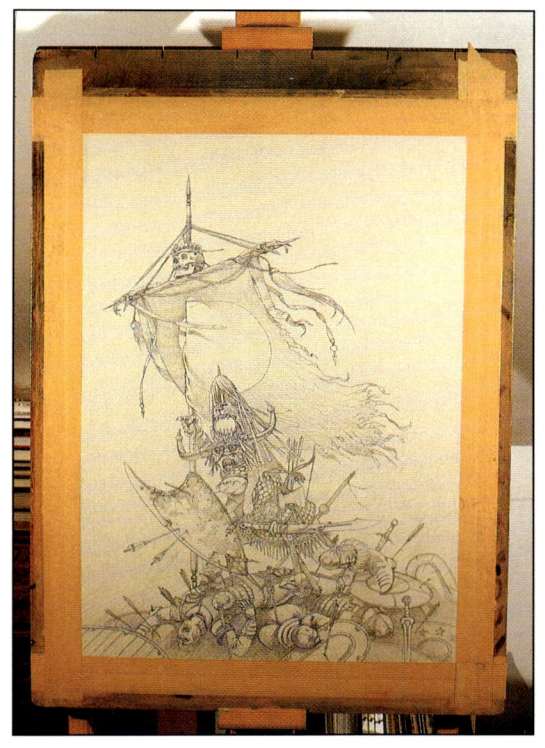

A The working drawing is transferred onto dry stretched paper and worked over with pencil.

B The background is to be done first so Frisk film is cut round figures and banner. Great care is needed not to cut through the paper.

C When you don't have to worry about clean edging it is possible to be much bolder with the background.

D The masking is removed to reveal perfectly clean edge round the foreground.

57

E Here I begin to bring out the form of the figures, using monochrome colour rendered to allow the paper's colour to show through.

F Work continued up into main figure. The advantage of coloured paper is that it can save a lot of underpainting.

G This is plainly seen in the development of the banner; the paper's own colour provides the highlights.

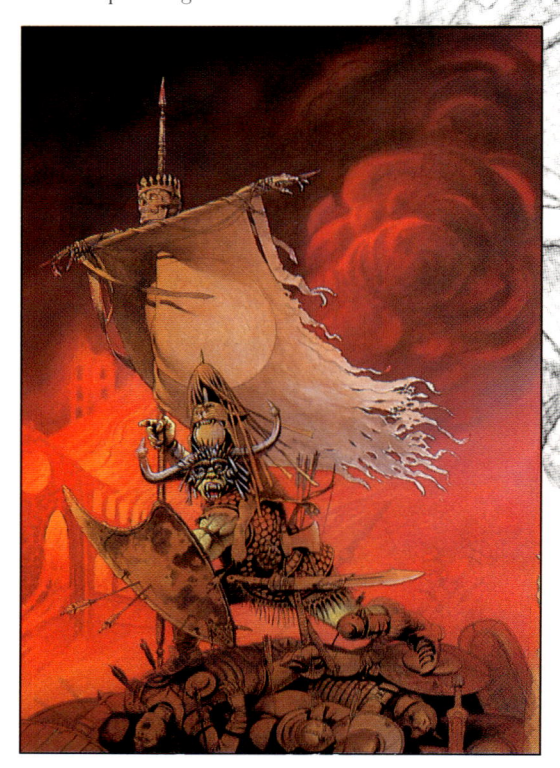

H I start to use opaque colour for the first time on the figures, picking out details on the orc's skin and helmet.

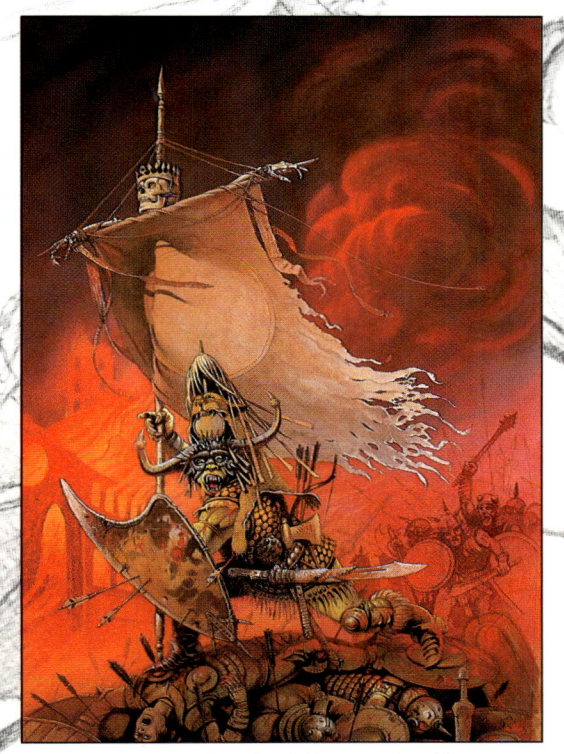

I Same thing continued, picking out details on fallen figures and armour. Note figures taking shape in the background.

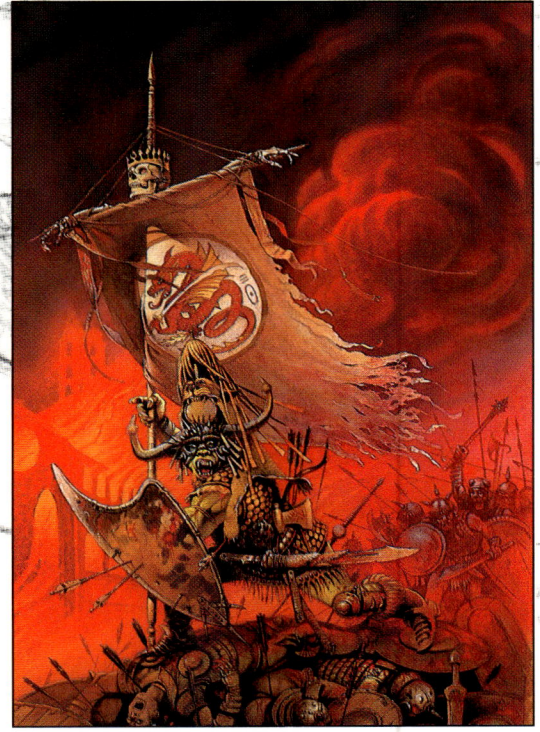

J The standard has been captured from the fallen good guy's army, customised with their king's skull complete with crown.

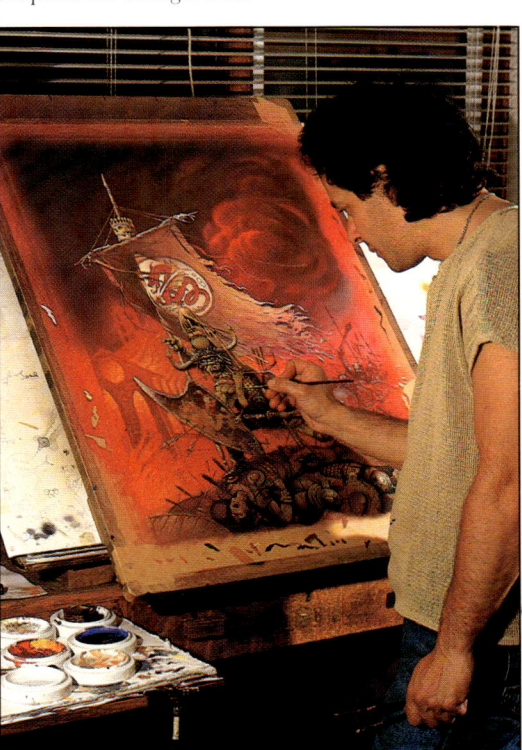

K Here you can see the size of the original painting. I usually stand for the broader work and sit for fine detail work.

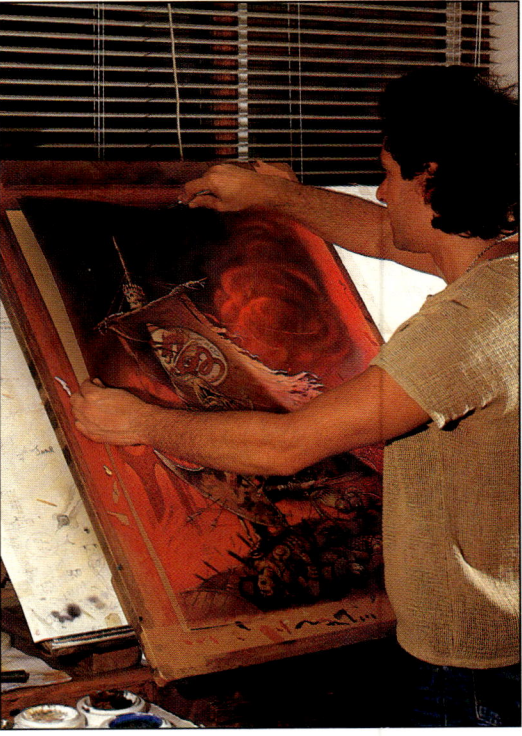

L Traumatic moment – cutting the picture free. After this no major corrections can be made without permanently wrinkling the paper.

60

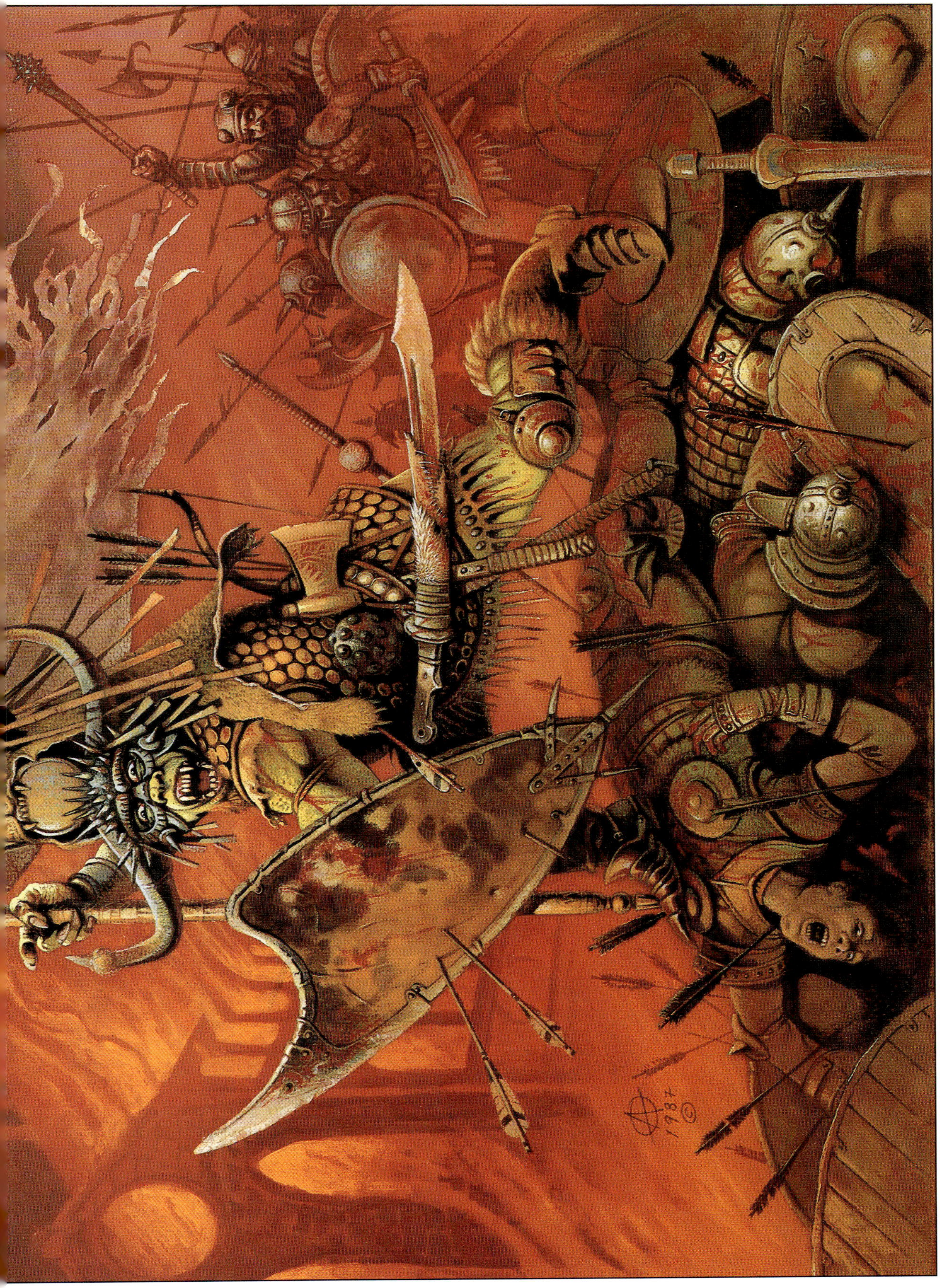

8 GRAPHIC ILLUSTRATION

Chris Achilleos is not only interested in Fantasy, Science Fiction or historical work. When the chance arises he also enjoys straightforward graphic work, where he can dust off his technical illustrator's skills.

The examples here were commissioned by an organisation that collects television news pictures from around the world and gathers them into an archive for the use of newsreel and documentary film-makers.

The first of the set was C, which was intended for advertising. To prepare for it Chris visited their centre on the outskirts of London to take reference photographs and generally get the feel of the place. What emerged was a fairly straight

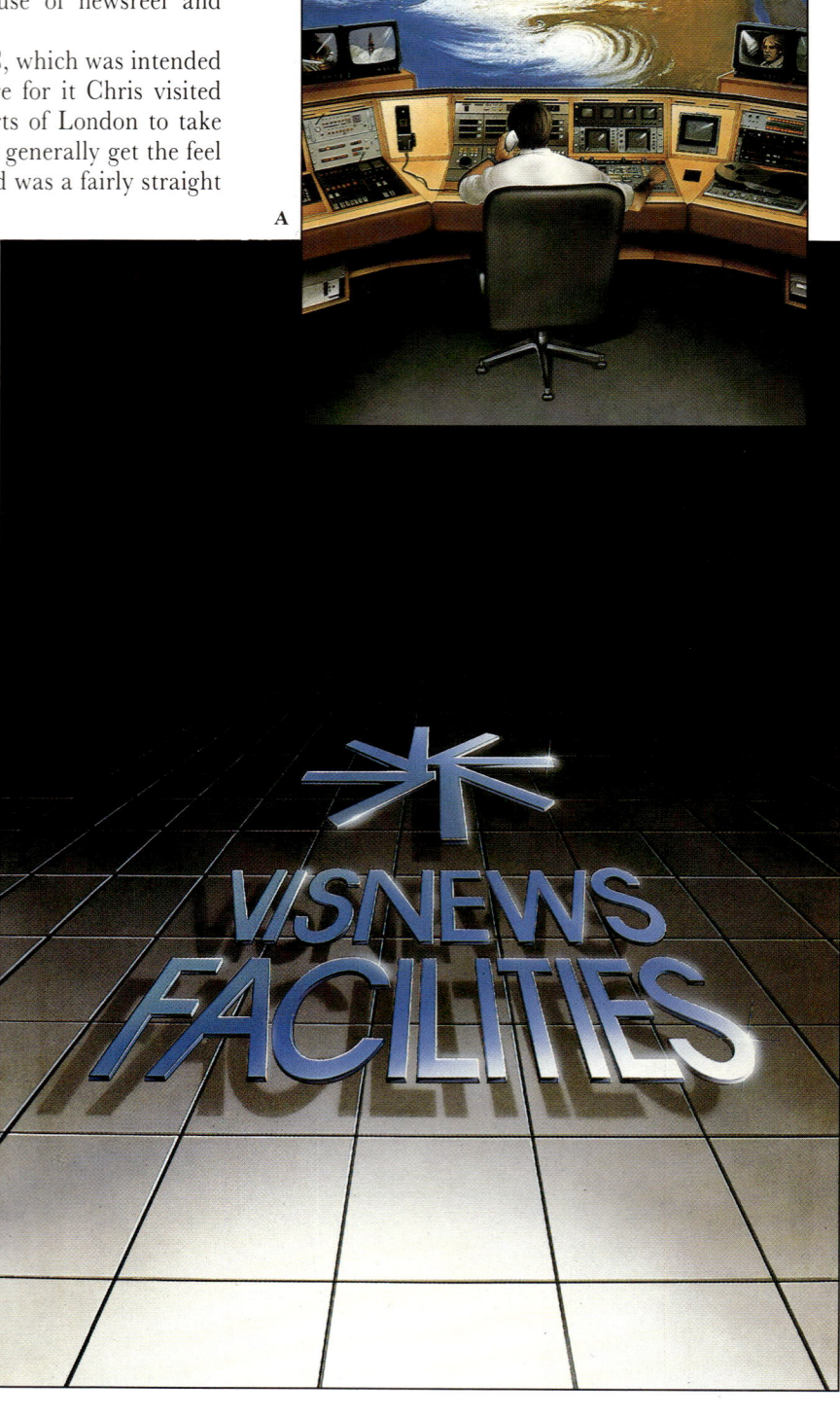

A

B

62

representation of the set-up – an underground complex below the city tuned to the outer world through a satellite dish.

In A he took a more conceptual approach, depicting Visnews as a spaceship with an overview of the planet. This was also done for advertising, while B was designed for a brochure cover, the perspective being Chris's idea. All were painted on hard line board with ink and gouache.

Earlier examples are shown on pages 64–65. The first of the top set was B, which was the result of a panic phone call from an old college friend, Roland Blunk, who is a freelance art director. He was then on commission for New Opportunity Press, providing covers for their publications, mostly magazines. He had just had to drop one on the eve of going to press because it illegally featured paper currency. Could Chris instantly come up with a substitute?

He agreed to try. The article was about students living on the breadline and after putting their heads together they came up with this concept.

C

This illustrated an article about the shrinking temporary job market. The concepts for this and the next three examples were Roland Blunk's.

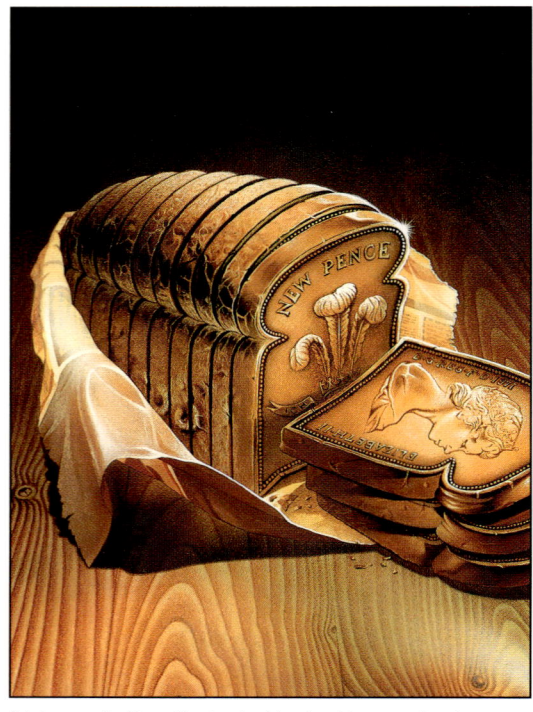

'Living on the Breadline' – the idea is a bit corny, but it works.

This was for a book about Biggin Hill airfield. I started painting my favourite aircraft, the Spitfire, but because someone forgot to mention it was mainly about the Battle of Britain era, I had to change them to an earlier model.

This cover was for one of a set of novels featuring bikers. Having no reference for BMWs from this angle I sketched one in a showroom, which felt like being back at college doing a still-life exercise.

The article to be illustrated was about the abolition of a step to higher education. To study splintering I smashed a piece of wood.

This was for a book called *Towards a Happier Retirement*, hence no more need for 9 and 5.

To match the format of the other covers, this was printed against a circular street map of a chase scene. I had to use reference books for the bike, whose plate number is that of the author's similar machine.

Here I avoided doing another motorbike, which I don't like anyway, having been almost killed by one as a kid in Cyprus.

9 HEAVY METAL

This was a concept drawing for a horde of barbarians and mutants. If some look familiar it is because they were borrowed from other pictures of mine that were similar to what the film-makers wanted.

68

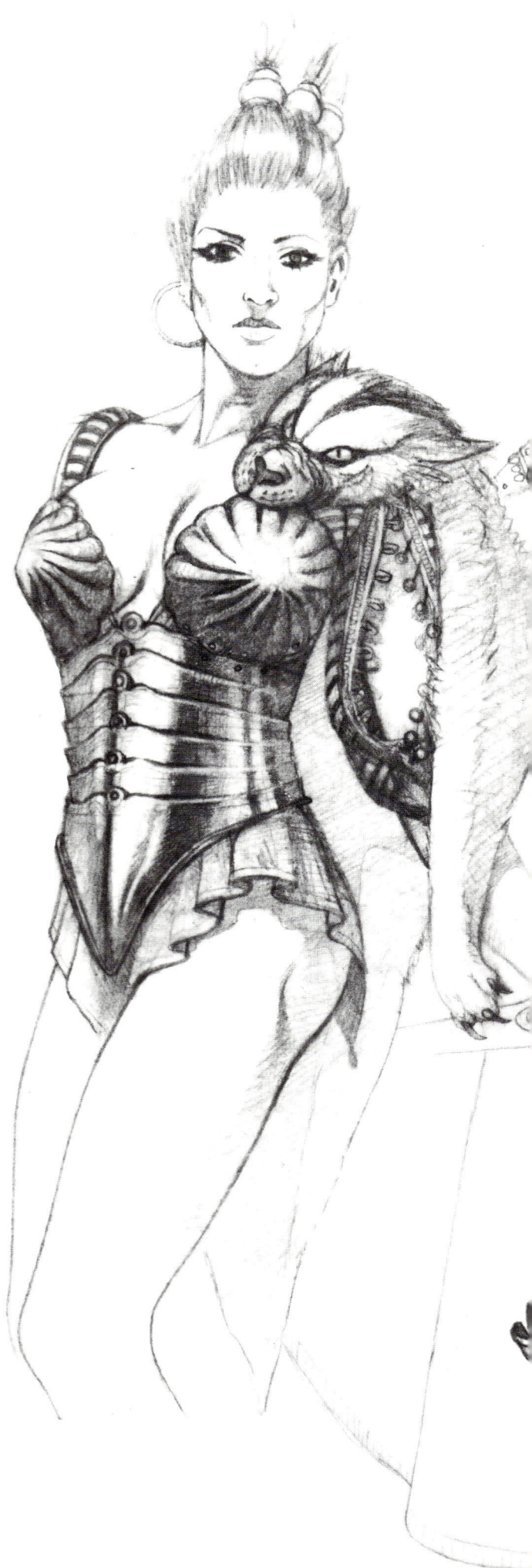

These sketches show early explorations into the character and costume of the heroine. Concept sketches like these do not need to be simple enough for animation, they just provide a starting point for ideas which can later be refined and stylised.

Here are some early explorations into Taarna's steed. The sketch on the lower far right was accepted, apart from the head. Something more cuddly and friendly was wanted, so I based the new head on a duck.

In the top row and on the left are some of the series of roughs I drew to find the right perspective for the cinema poster. There are a lot more!

Most illustrators might be tempted to sell their grandmothers to get into conceptual designing for films and Chris is no exception (though luckily his family loyalties have yet to be put to the test). His first chance came at the beginning of the Eighties, when he was asked to contribute ideas to a Fantasy sequence in the *Heavy Metal* film, which is made up of several self-contained stories within the framework of another which ties them all together.

The job involved providing concept sketches for various general scenes and incidental characters, but his main work was on the character and costume of the heroine, Taarna, and her flying charger. The brief called for a suit of armour, but somewhere along the line this was forgotten and Chris's design was whittled away to almost nothing. Both characters were also drastically simplified for animation purposes, but Chris's talent for dynamic realism was given full rein in the film's publicity poster, shown here.

To get the bird's head right he made two Plasticine models, one to get the film-makers' approval and the other to work from in the final picture. For Taarna he asked a friend, Pam, to pose for him, a rare occurrence, but in this case he felt he really had to get the pose right.

Recently Chris had a call asking if he might be interested in doing similar work for a new Fantasy film by George Lucas. After considering it deeply for several microseconds he said yes and later had a call from Lucas himself, inviting him to Elstree studios, where much of the work was being done.

The quality that had most attracted Lucas to Chris Achilleos' work is his ability to imagine costumes that are both exotic and practical. In the event, though, he was called on to design far more than the main characters' costumes and produced wide-ranging sketches of both the good and evil empires. Also he designed a complete culture of little people, who feature strongly in the story. Unfortunately we cannot show examples here because of the possibility of this book appearing before the film, which is to be called *Willow*.

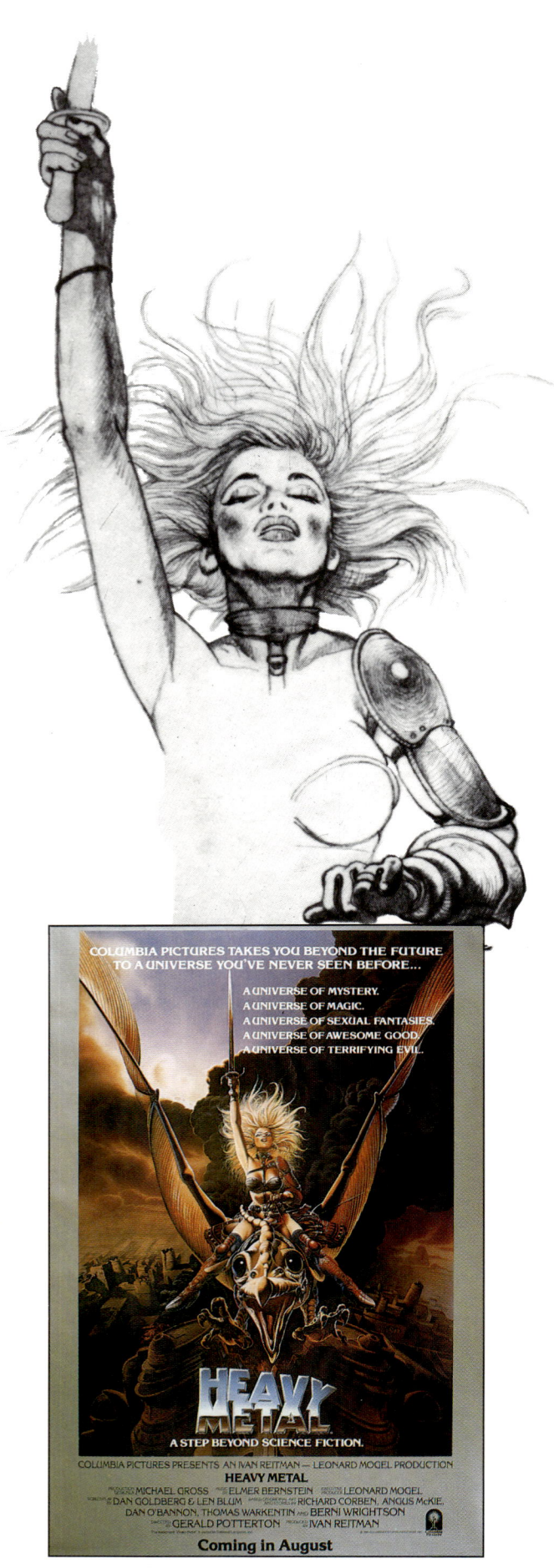

THE FILM POSTER

TAARNA

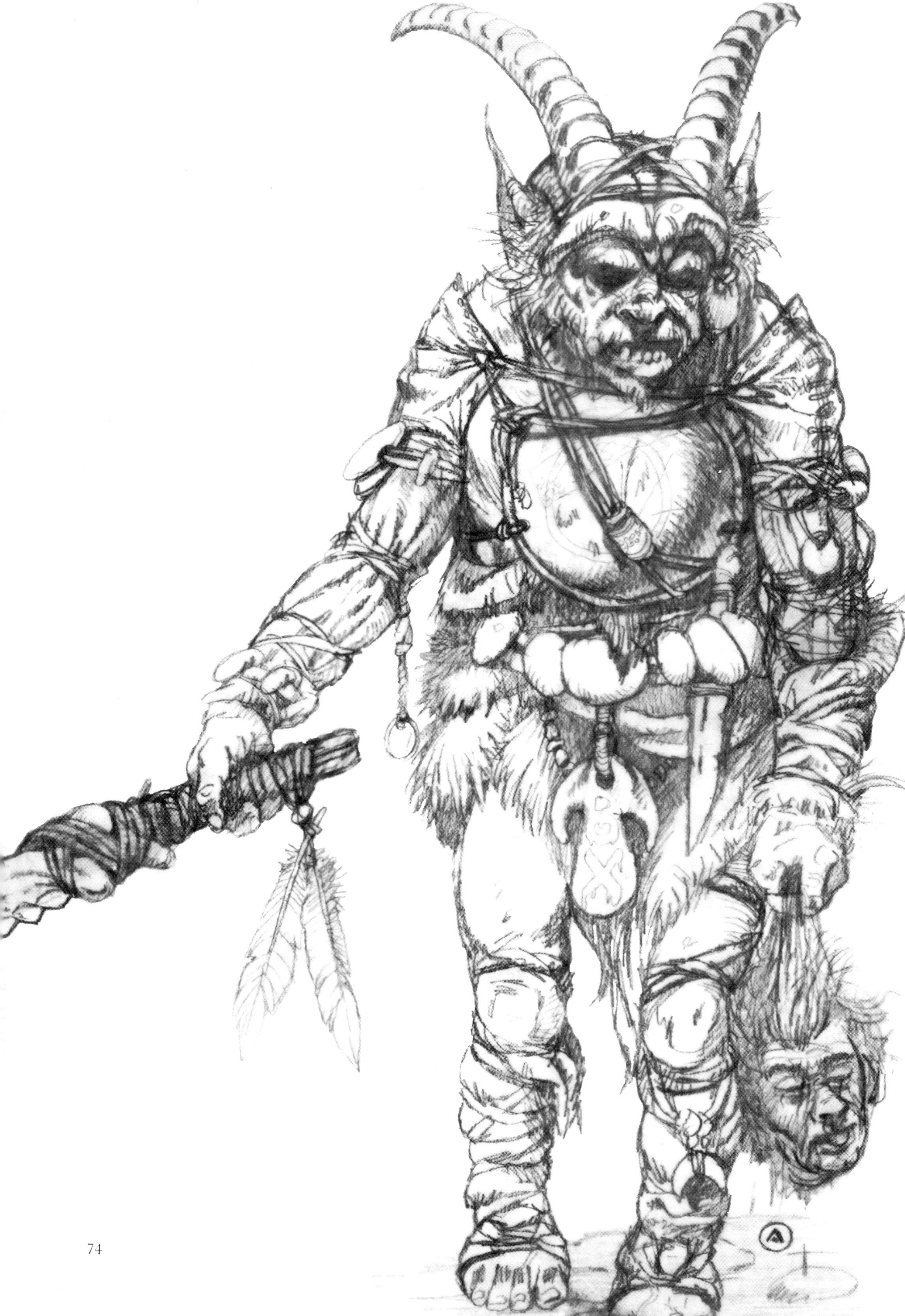

When commissioned for the Taarna section of the film Heavy Metal, I was asked to work on all the main characters, but later this work was passed on to others so that I could concentrate on the heroine and her steed.

The mutant barbarian on the left was based on a Neanderthal man. I was tempted to put a Volkswagen logo on the hubcap strapped to his chest, but could not for obvious reasons.

On the right is an episode featuring one of Taarna's allies and her enchanted sword.

STAR TREK

10

These cover illustrations were for a series of twelve books each containing up to five stories from the television series. Great care was taken to get the colour and details right in order to avoid stirring the wrath of fanatical Trekkies.

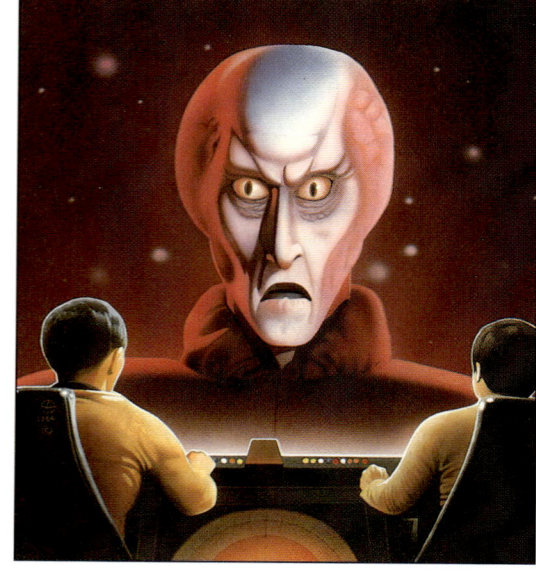

THE CORBOMITE MANEUVER

WHERE NO MAN HAS GONE BEFORE

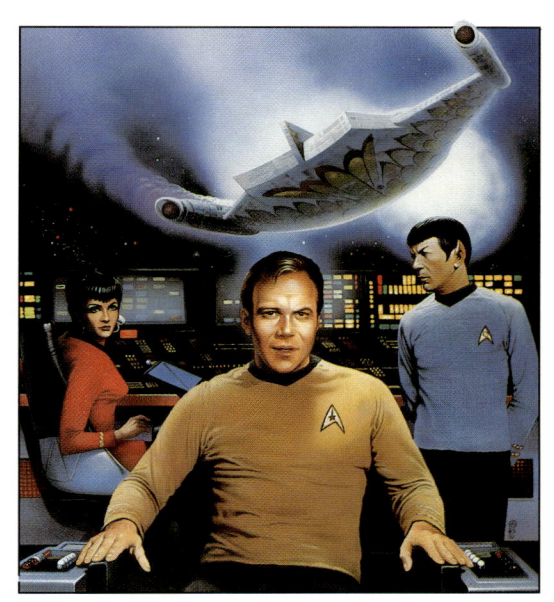

BALANCE OF TERROR

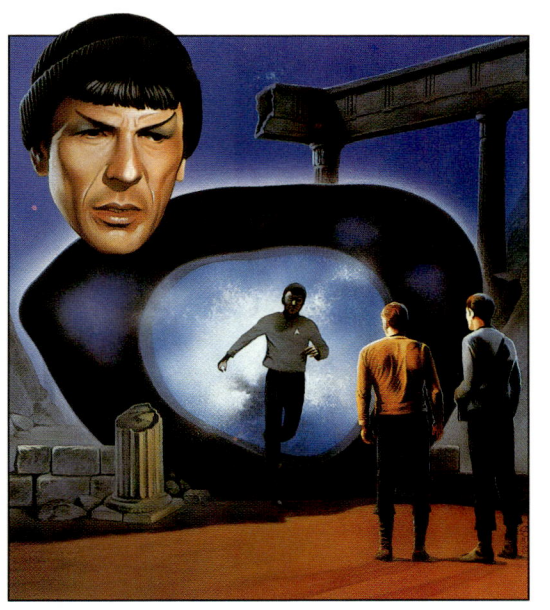

THE CITY ON THE EDGE OF FOREVER

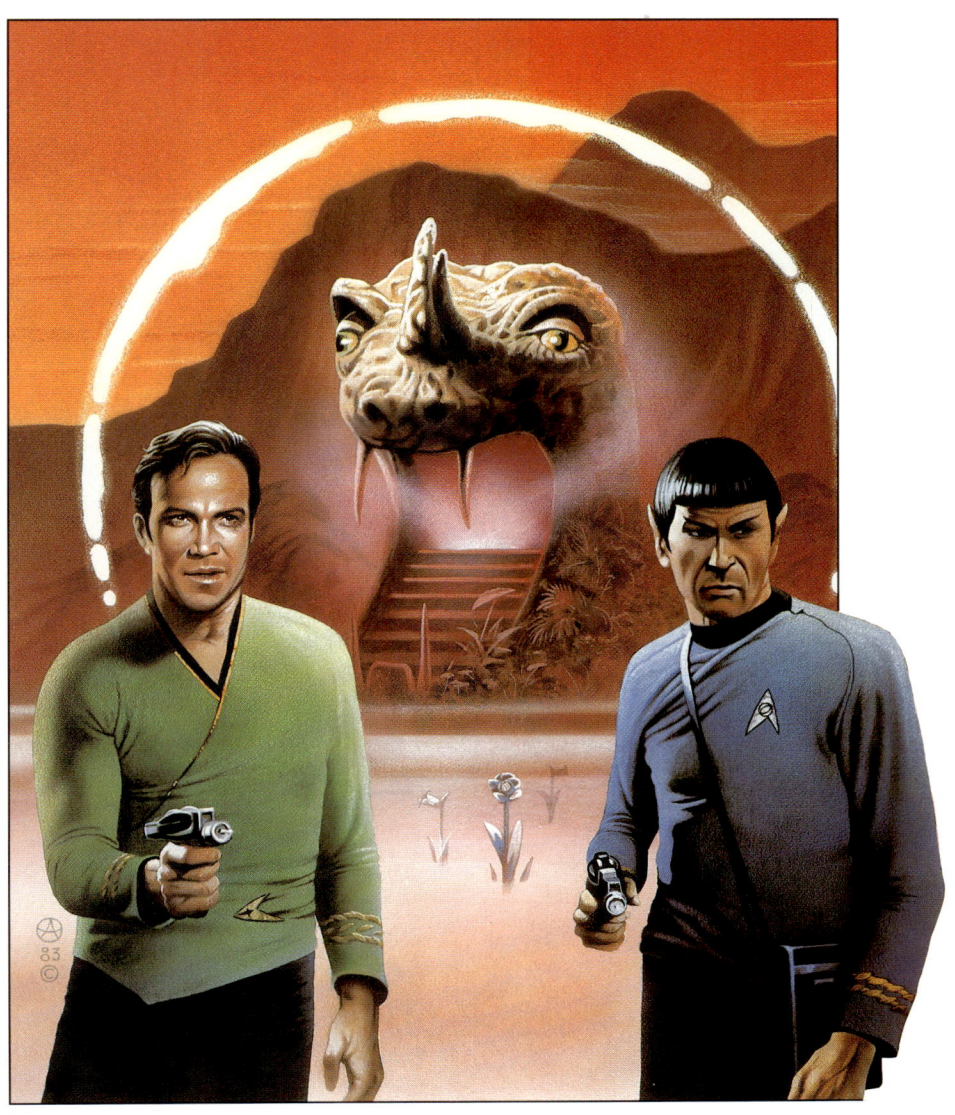

THE APPLE

77

The problem with this series was that each book contained so many good stories that it was hard to choose one for the cover. On one or two occasions all the dull stories were lumped together and it was just as hard to find enthusiasm for any.

On the far right I chose the headstone scene because, in the TV episode, the second pilot for the series, the captain's name appears as 'James R. Kirk'. I wanted to spotlight the later change.

78

JAMES T. KIRK
C1277.1 to 1818.7

THE IMMUNITY
SYNDROME

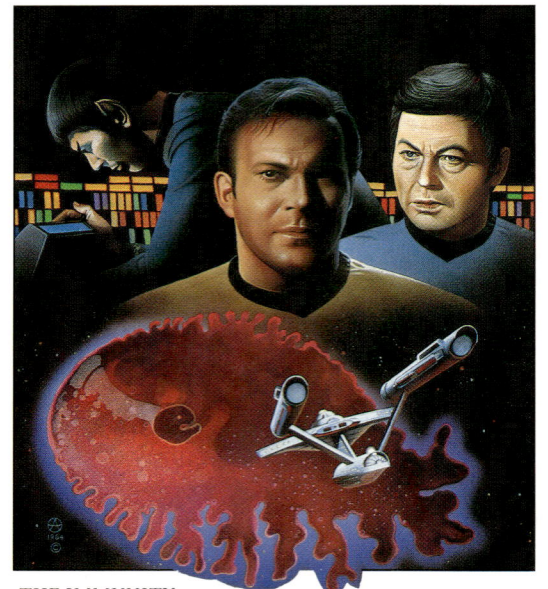

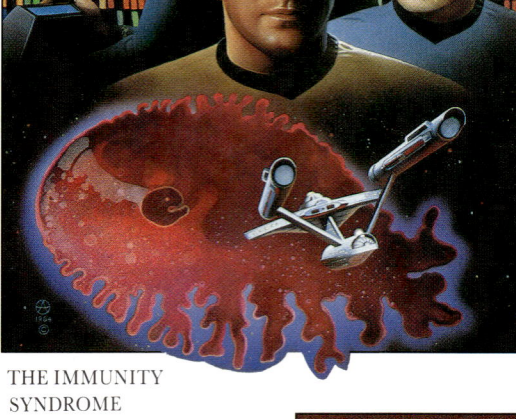

WHO MOURNS FOR ADONAIS

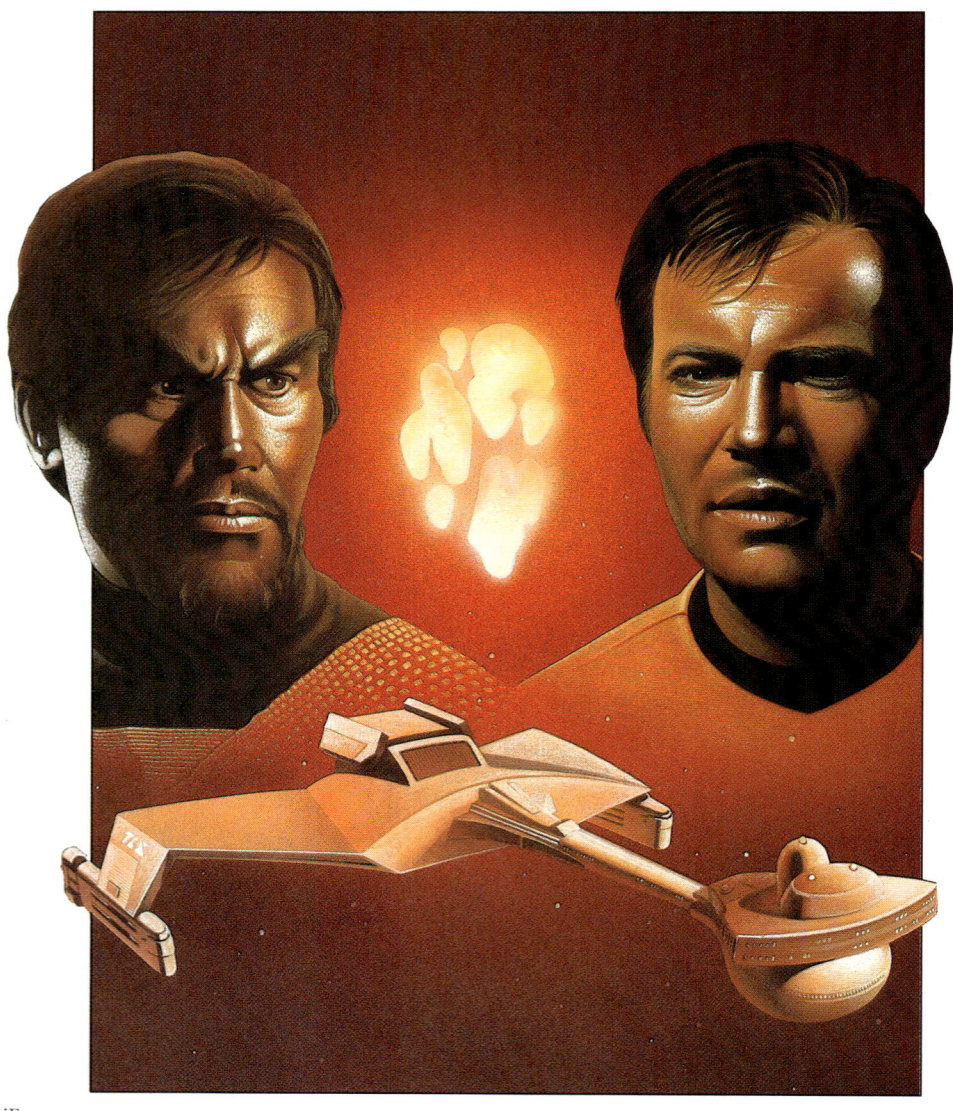

THE DAY OF THE DOVE

80

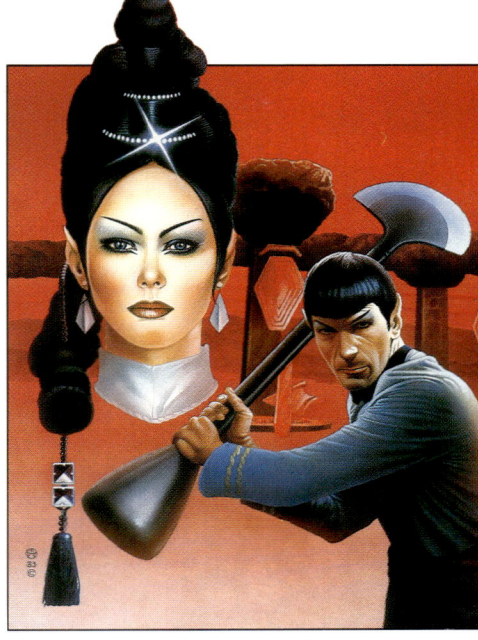

ALL OUR YESTERDAYS

AMOK TIME

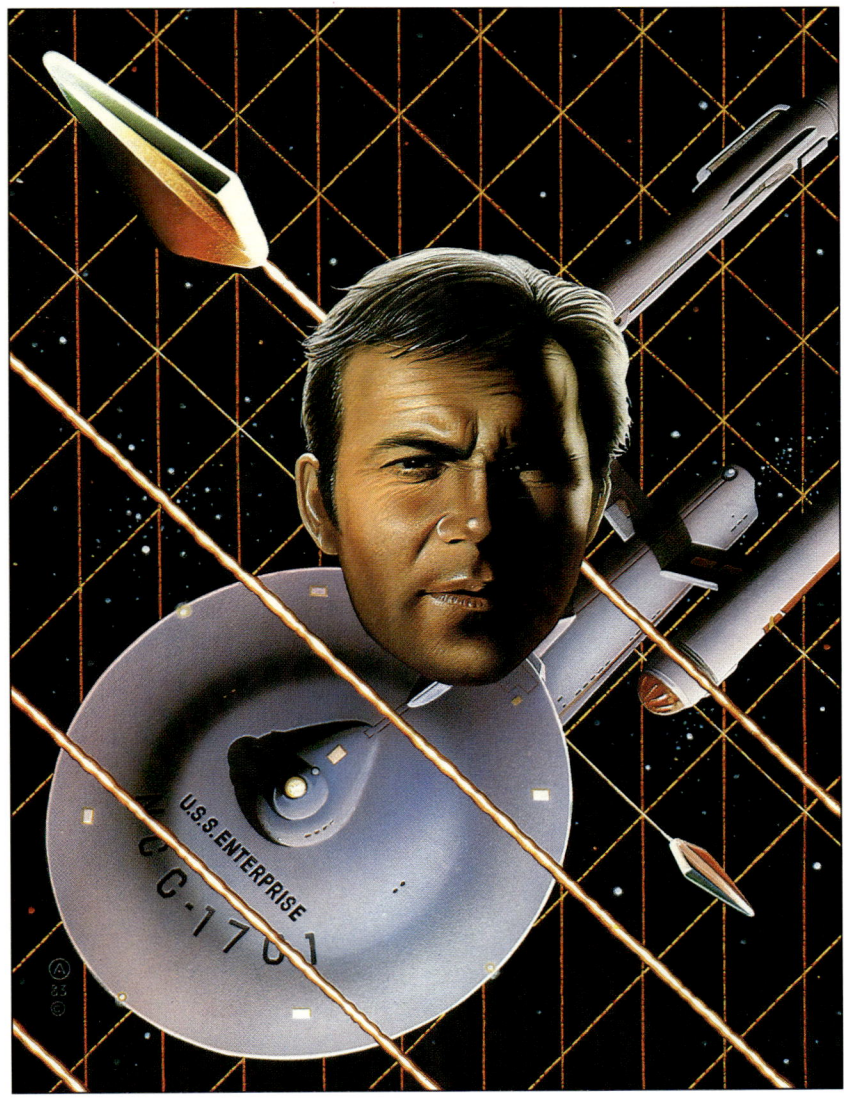

THE THALIAN WEB

81

11 FILM POSTERS

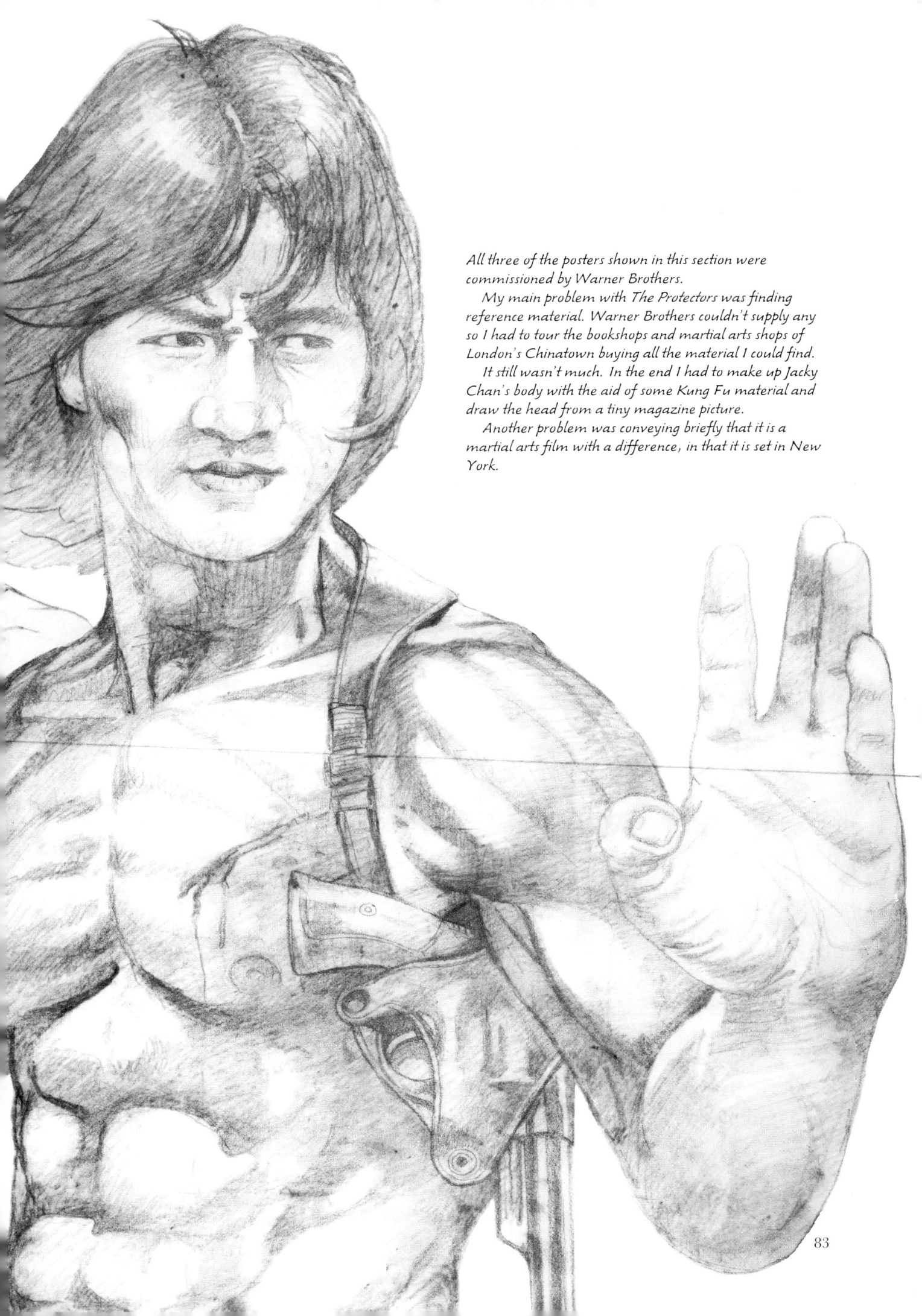

All three of the posters shown in this section were commissioned by Warner Brothers.

My main problem with The Protectors *was finding reference material. Warner Brothers couldn't supply any so I had to tour the bookshops and martial arts shops of London's Chinatown buying all the material I could find.*

It still wasn't much. In the end I had to make up Jacky Chan's body with the aid of some Kung Fu material and draw the head from a tiny magazine picture.

Another problem was conveying briefly that it is a martial arts film with a difference, in that it is set in New York.

THE PROTECTOR

MARINE ISSUE
In this I aimed for the effect of a military recruiting poster of the 1940s, hence his static pose and the flat colour of his uniform. The gun was invented for the film and looks like a toy, so I didn't want to use it. In my rough I substituted a real one, but the film-makers insisted on me using theirs, which I am still unhappy about because it ruins the whole picture.

85

1984

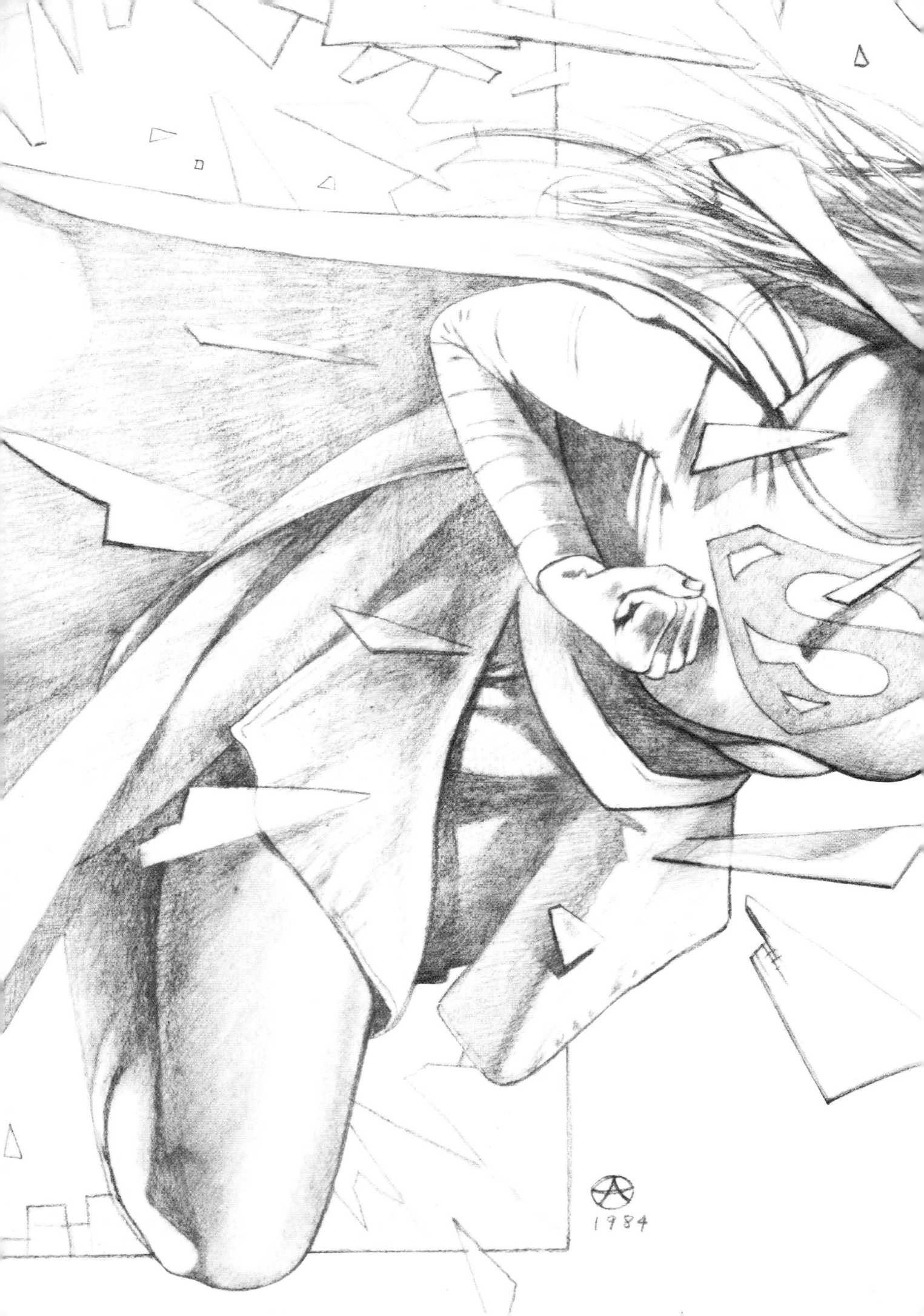

For this commission I submitted several large drawings from which I expected to be asked for one painting. Instead I was asked for three.
For the picture of Supergirl bursting through the mirror I did a detailed portrait of Faye Dunaway on one piece of paper and Supergirl on another, the two were then combined for the painting.
In the end my posters were not used because the studio sold the movie while I was still working on them.

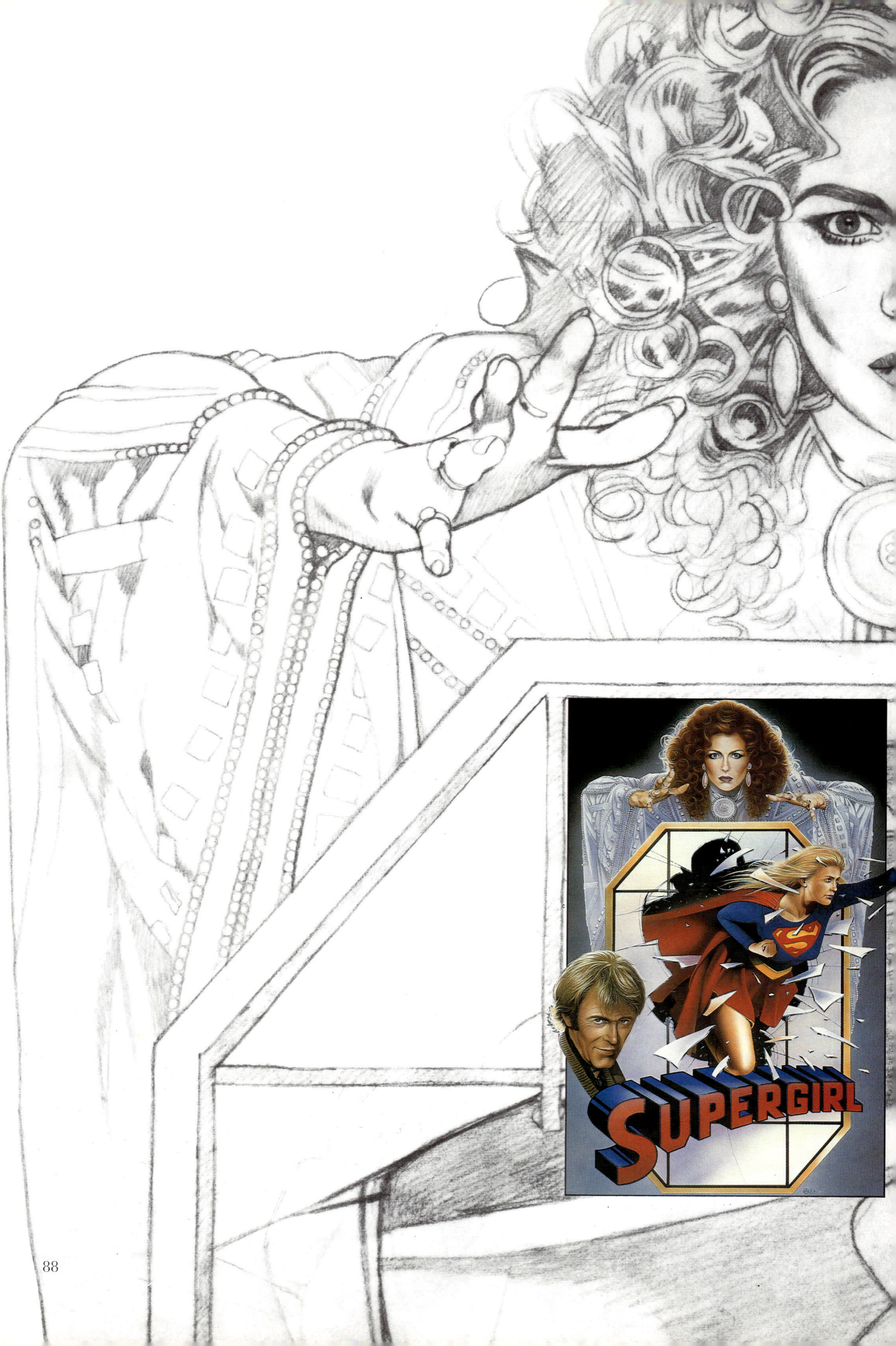
SUPERGIRL

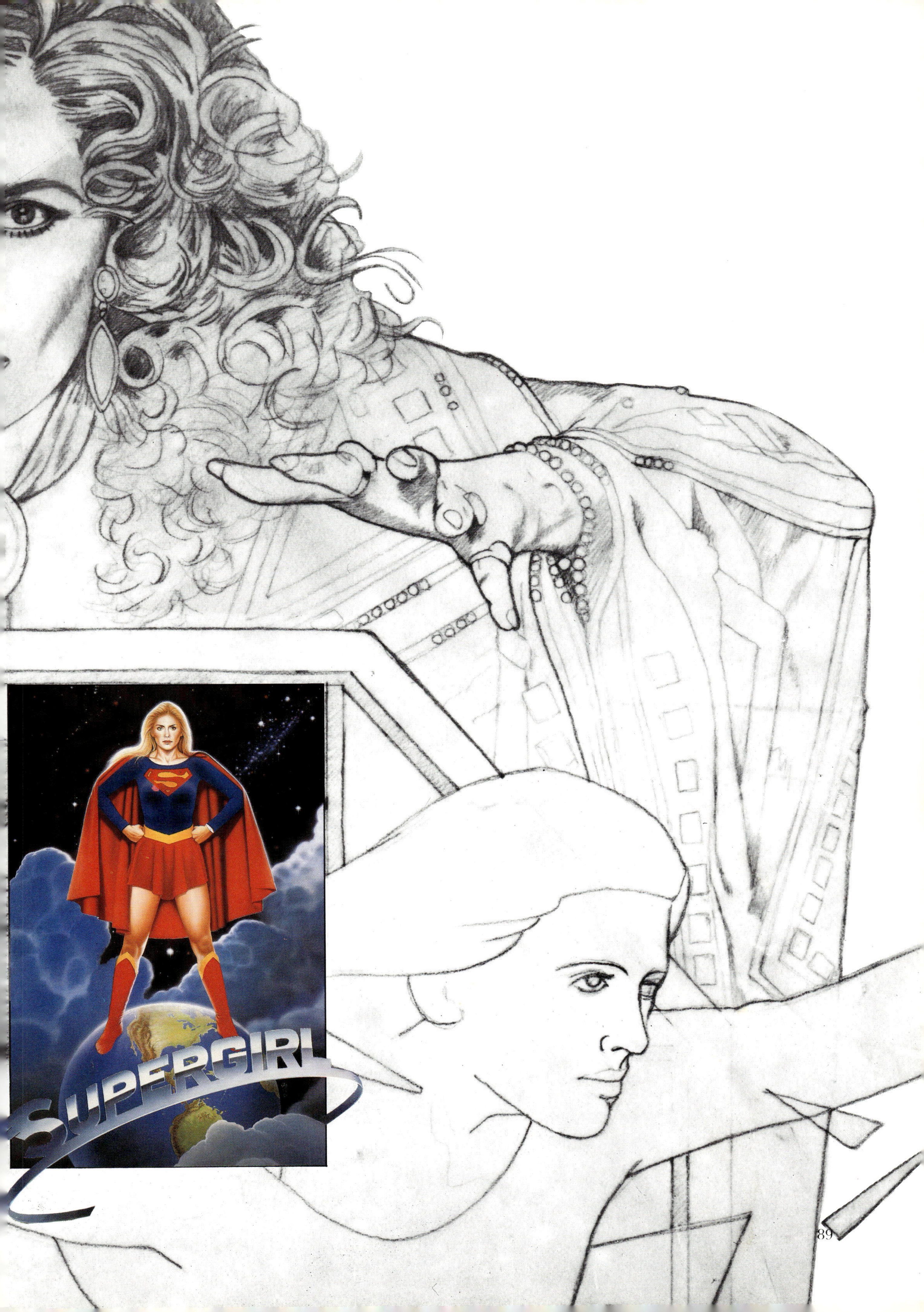
SUPERGIRL

12 AMAZONS

These three heads were done separately on tracing paper and placed on top of the body drawing to see which would look best. This way I saved a lot of time and effort.

A

B

Shown here are all the drawings leading up to the painting stage. The original concept is shown in A. B shows the intermediate stage, the centre line being there to help enlarge it to the final scale.

On the right is the final working drawing, same size as original.

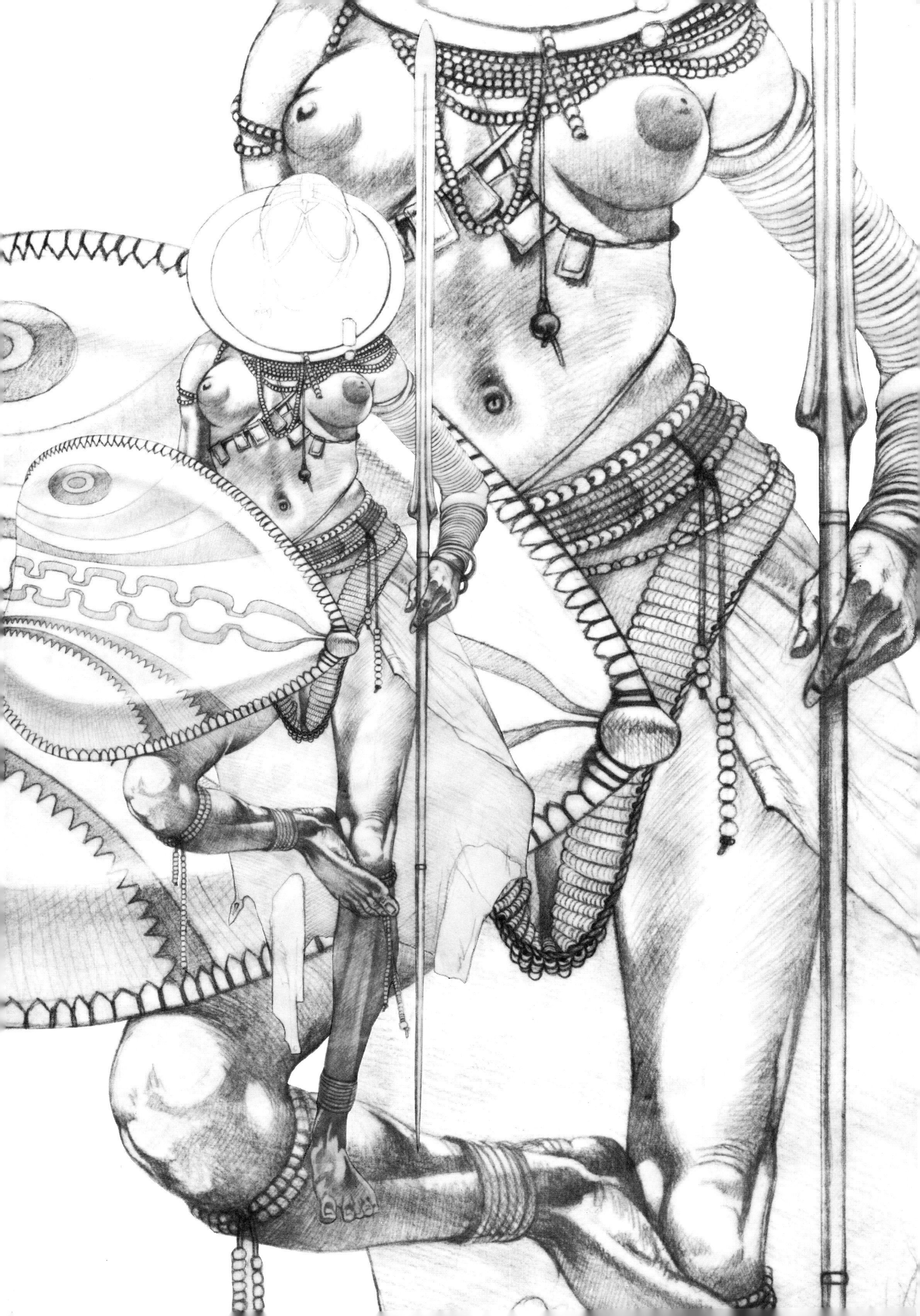

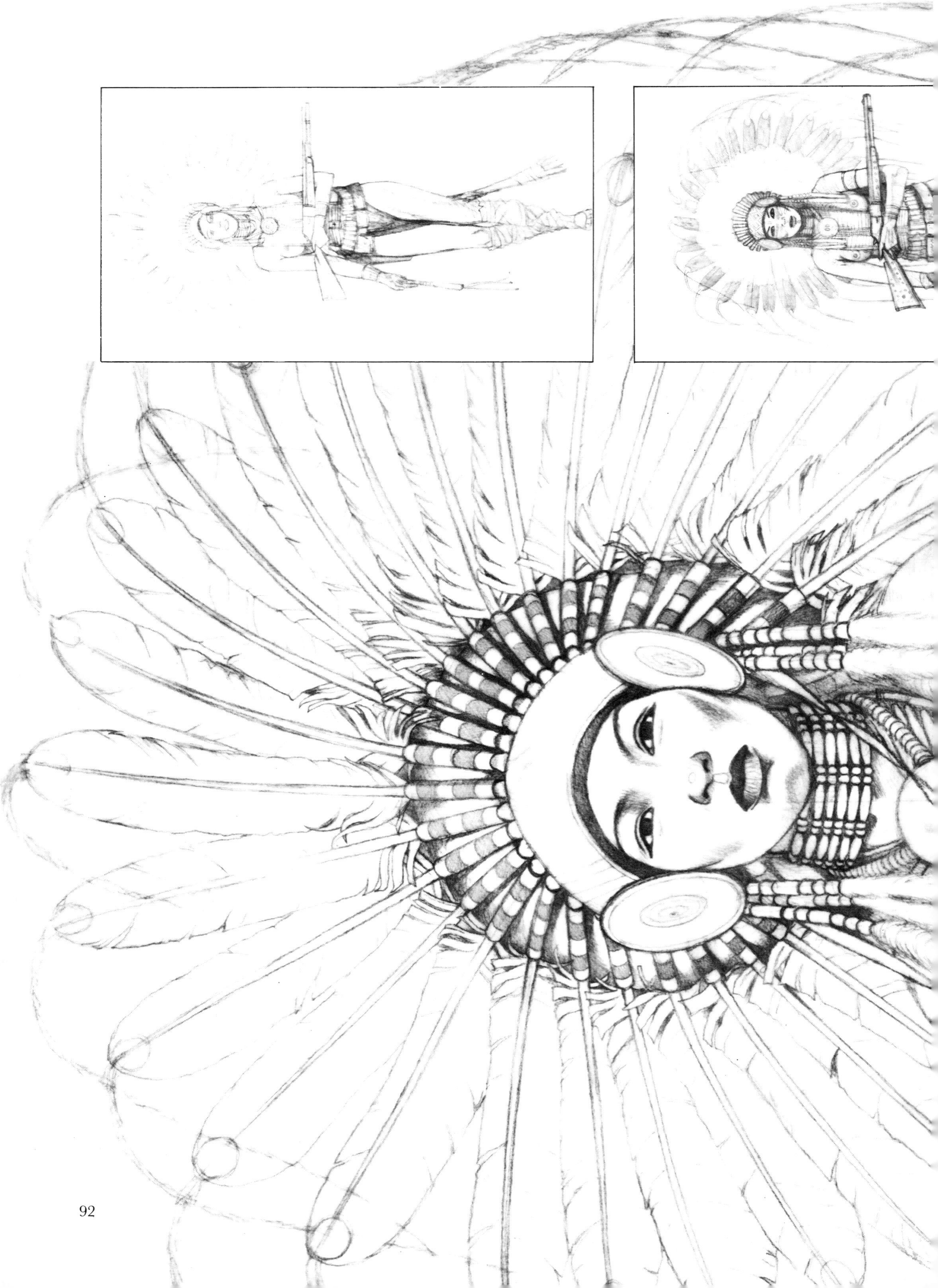

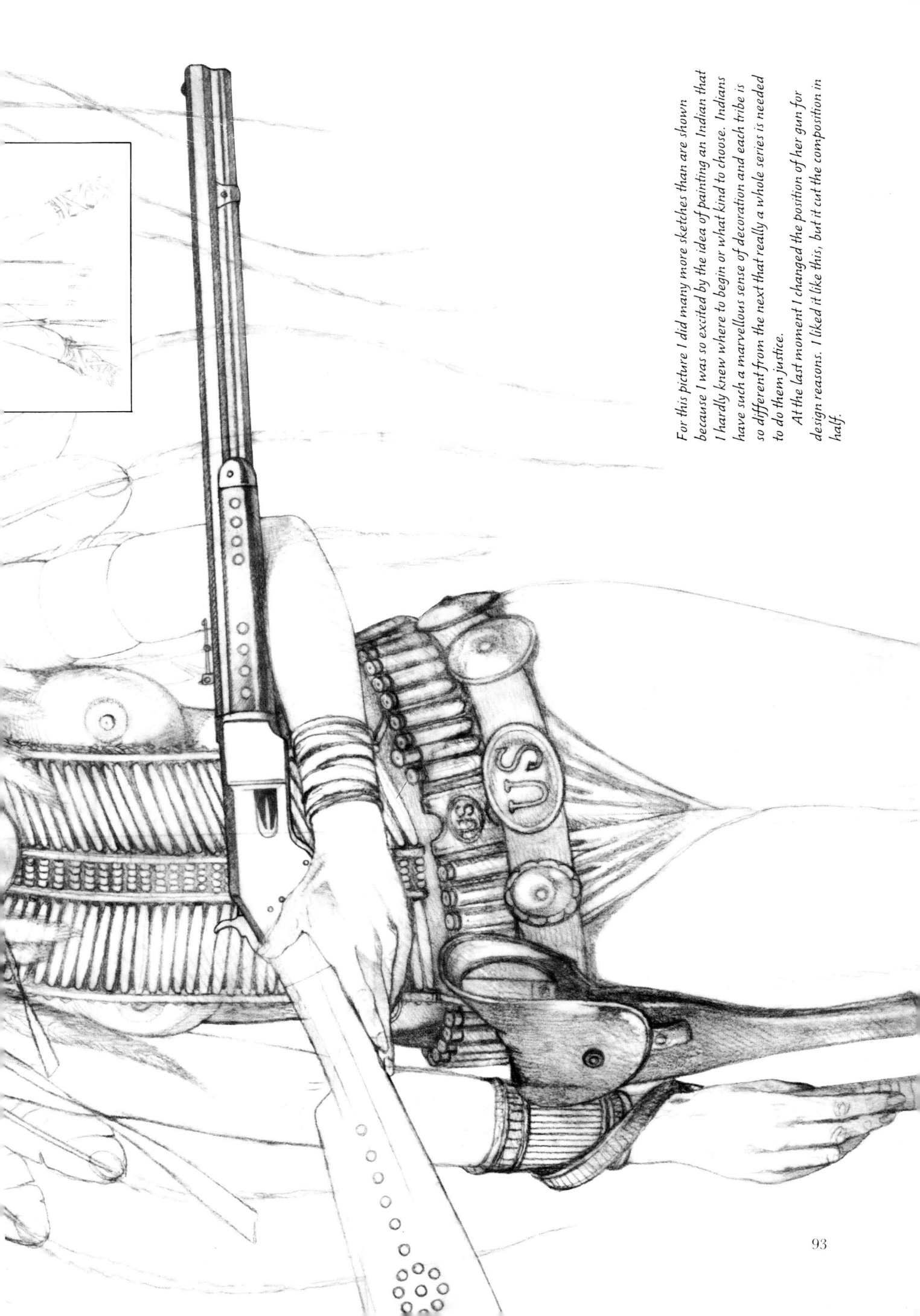

For this picture I did many more sketches than are shown because I was so excited by the idea of painting an Indian that I hardly knew where to begin or what kind to choose. Indians have such a marvellous sense of decoration and each tribe is so different from the next that really a whole series is needed to do them justice.

At the last moment I changed the position of her gun for design reasons. I liked it like this, but it cut the composition in half.

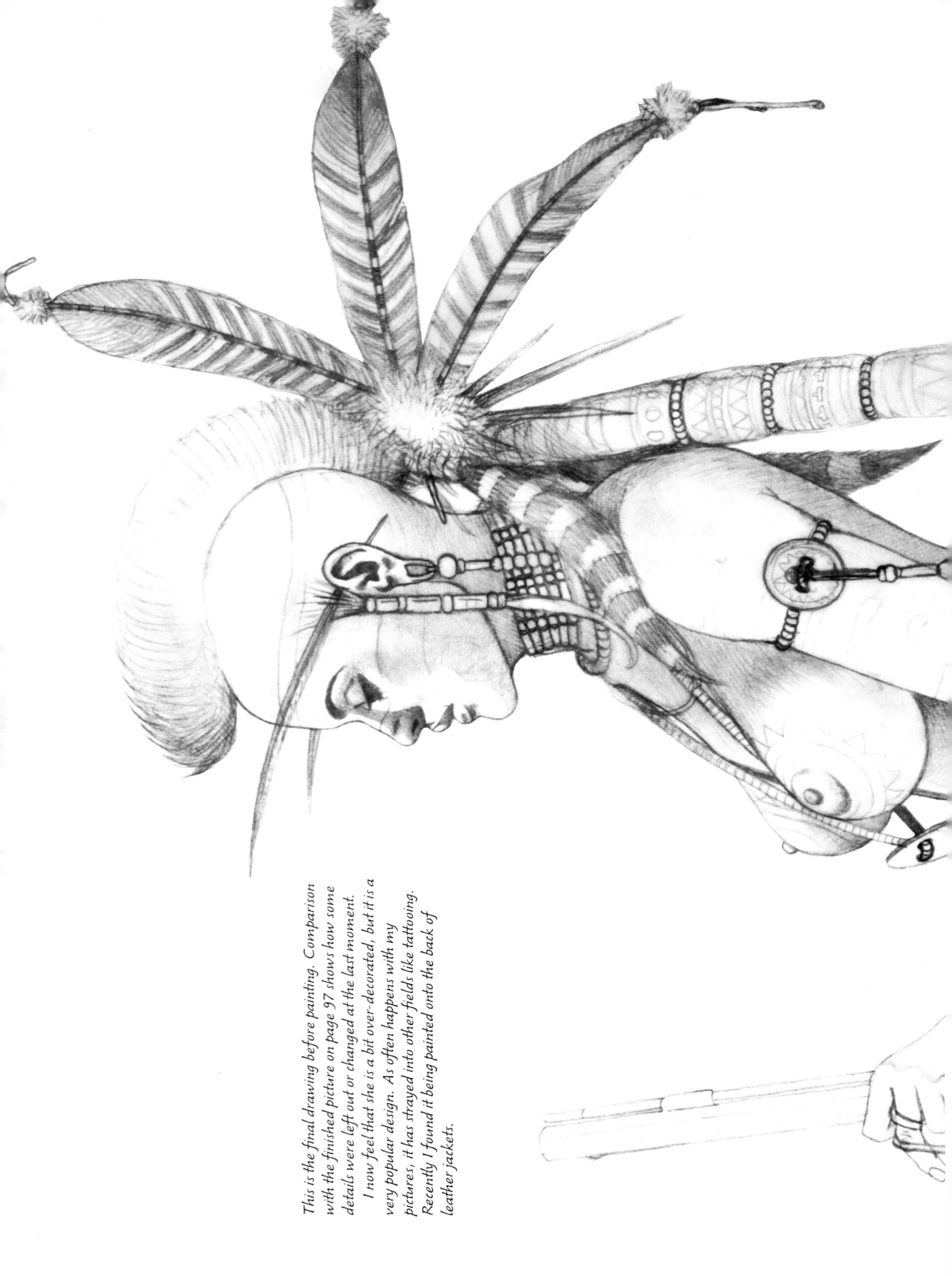

This is the final drawing before painting. Comparison with the finished picture on page 97 shows how some details were left out or changed at the last moment.

I now feel that she is a bit over-decorated, but it is a very popular design. As often happens with my pictures, it has strayed into other fields like tattooing. Recently I found it being painted onto the back of leather jackets.

95

CHEYENNE MODEL
This model was produced under licence by Fine Art Castings. It stands about 15 cm tall and is the first of a series to be cast in heavy metal. The models come bare so they can be hand-painted. Some models like this are sculpted rather crudely, so I kept a careful eye on the development of the prototype.

I have a recent pencil drawing of an Apache if anyone out there would like to commission the painting.

MAASAI CHEYENNE MODEL

CHEYENNE

REDSKIN

97

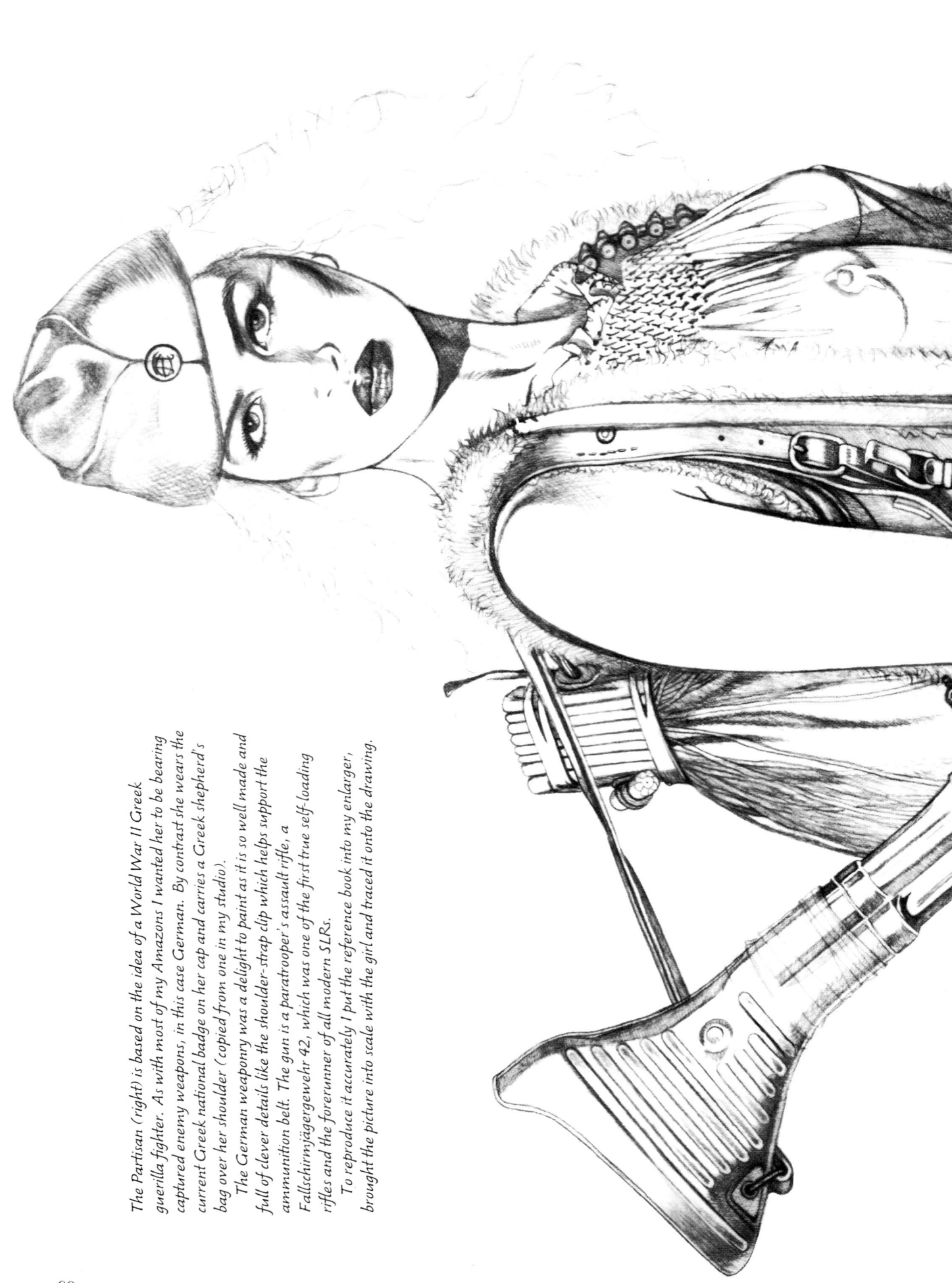

The Partisan (right) is based on the idea of a World War II Greek guerilla fighter. As with most of my Amazons I wanted her to be bearing captured enemy weapons, in this case German. By contrast she wears the current Greek national badge on her cap and carries a Greek shepherd's bag over her shoulder (copied from one in my studio).

The German weaponry was a delight to paint as it is so well made and full of clever details like the shoulder-strap clip which helps support the ammunition belt. The gun is a paratrooper's assault rifle, a Fallschirmjägergewehr 42, which was one of the first true self-loading rifles and the forerunner of all modern SLRs.

To reproduce it accurately I put the reference book into my enlarger, brought the picture into scale with the girl and traced it onto the drawing.

99

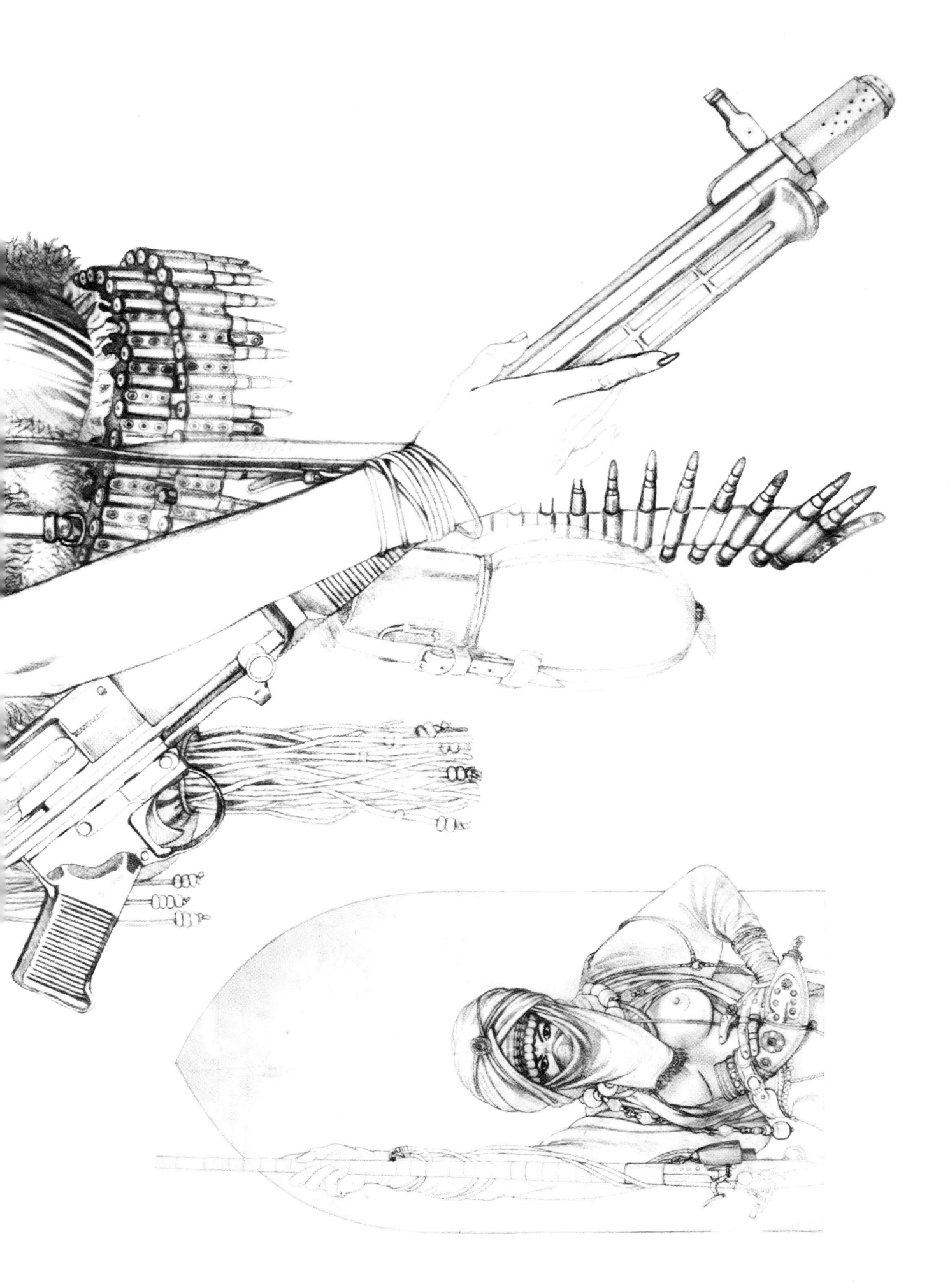

HAREM GUARD
This was a great chance to indulge my interest in Orientalism,
about which I have a shelf-full of books.

JUNGLE GIRL
This picture along with some others was carried off to Los Angeles by a supposed friend under false pretences. He and all my pictures have vanished, so if anyone spots the original could they please let me know.

THE PARTISAN
This was almost a technical exercise because of the variety of different textures brought together – gunmetal, wood, soft skin, hair, etc. They were unified by an overall earthy colour. I am aware that a real-life partisan would hardly have looked like this, but I felt compelled to make her as glamorous as Hollywood would have done in the 1940s and 50s.

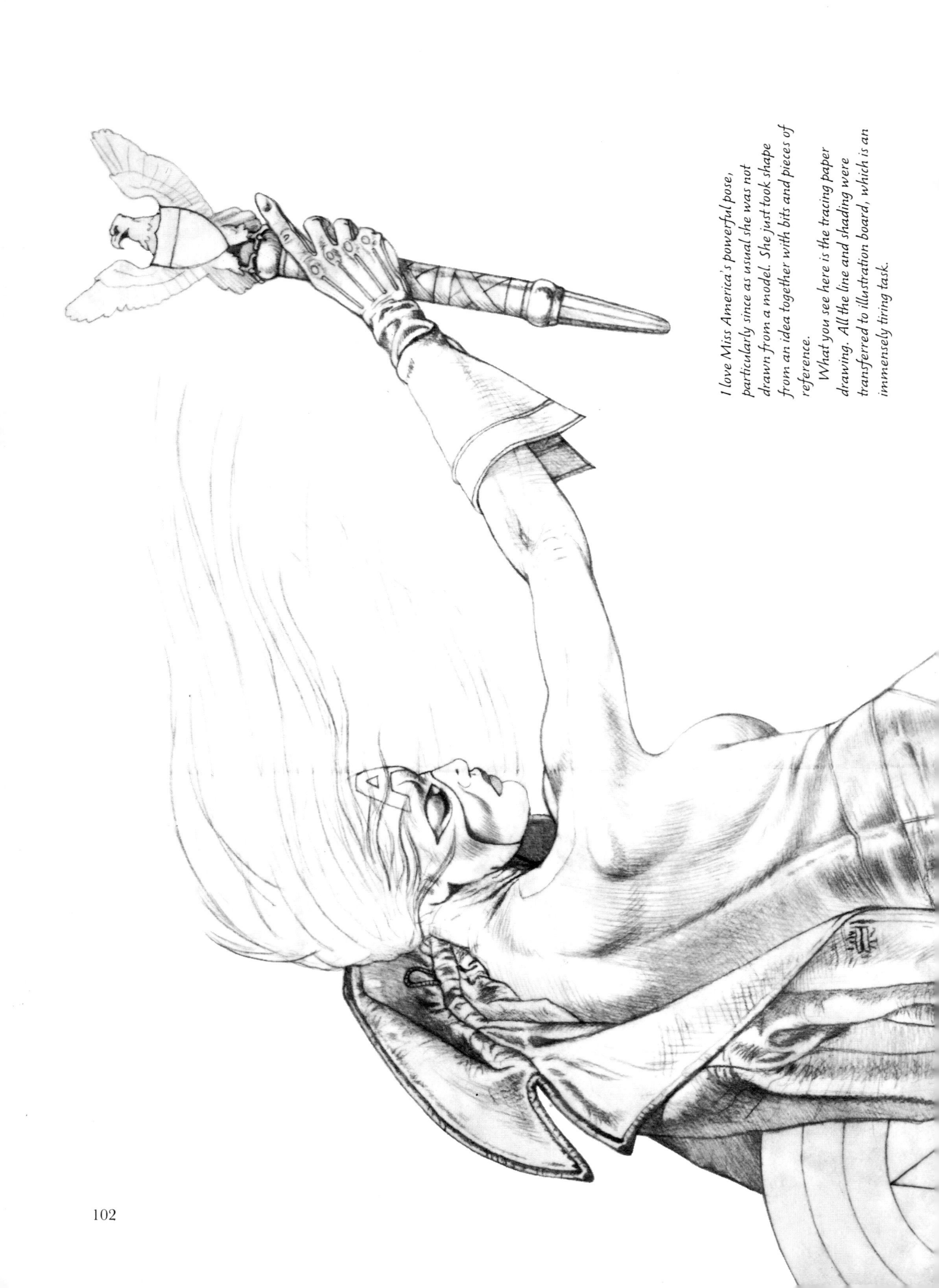

I love Miss America's powerful pose, particularly since as usual she was not drawn from a model. She just took shape from an idea together with bits and pieces of reference.

What you see here is the tracing paper drawing. All the line and shading were transferred to illustration board, which is an immensely tiring task.

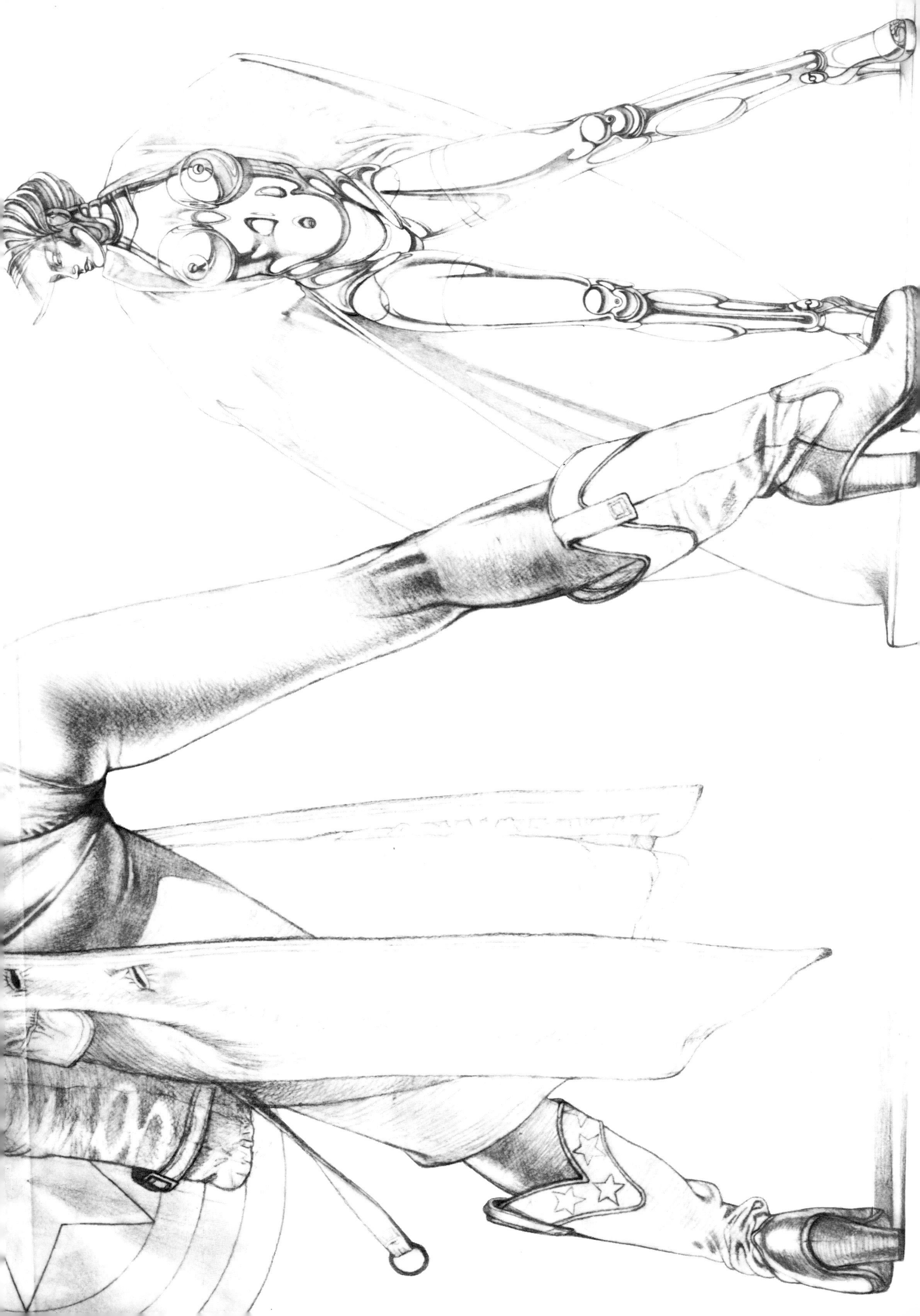

MISS AMERICA

(centre) STARSHIP CAPTAIN (drawing)
same size as original

(below) MODEL 2000
I love painting metal and I love painting women. Here the two came together. My main problem was imagining where the red cloak would reflect in the chrome, which I solved purely in my head.

(below left) STARSHIP CAPTAIN
There is a common misconception about the girl in this picture. Her hands are not meant to be claws. The effect being aimed at was of hard plastic armour over soft gloves.

13 SUPER CREEPS

This commission was for the cover of a game based on The Lord of the Rings. Because of the subject I put far more into it than was strictly called for.

One of my most difficult drawings, it is a patchwork of different bits stuck over each other after shuffling the figures around to find the right composition.

THE HOST OF MORDOR

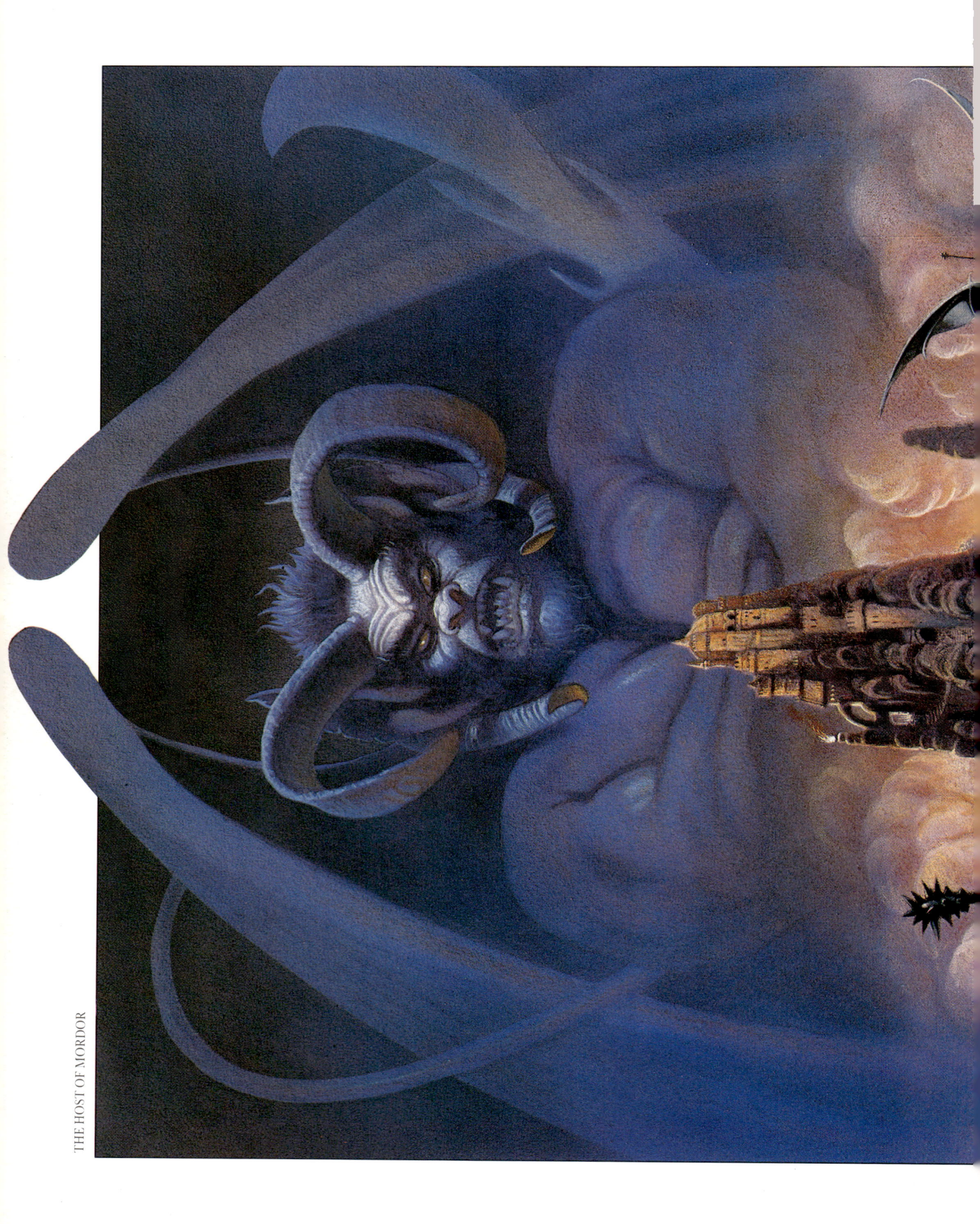

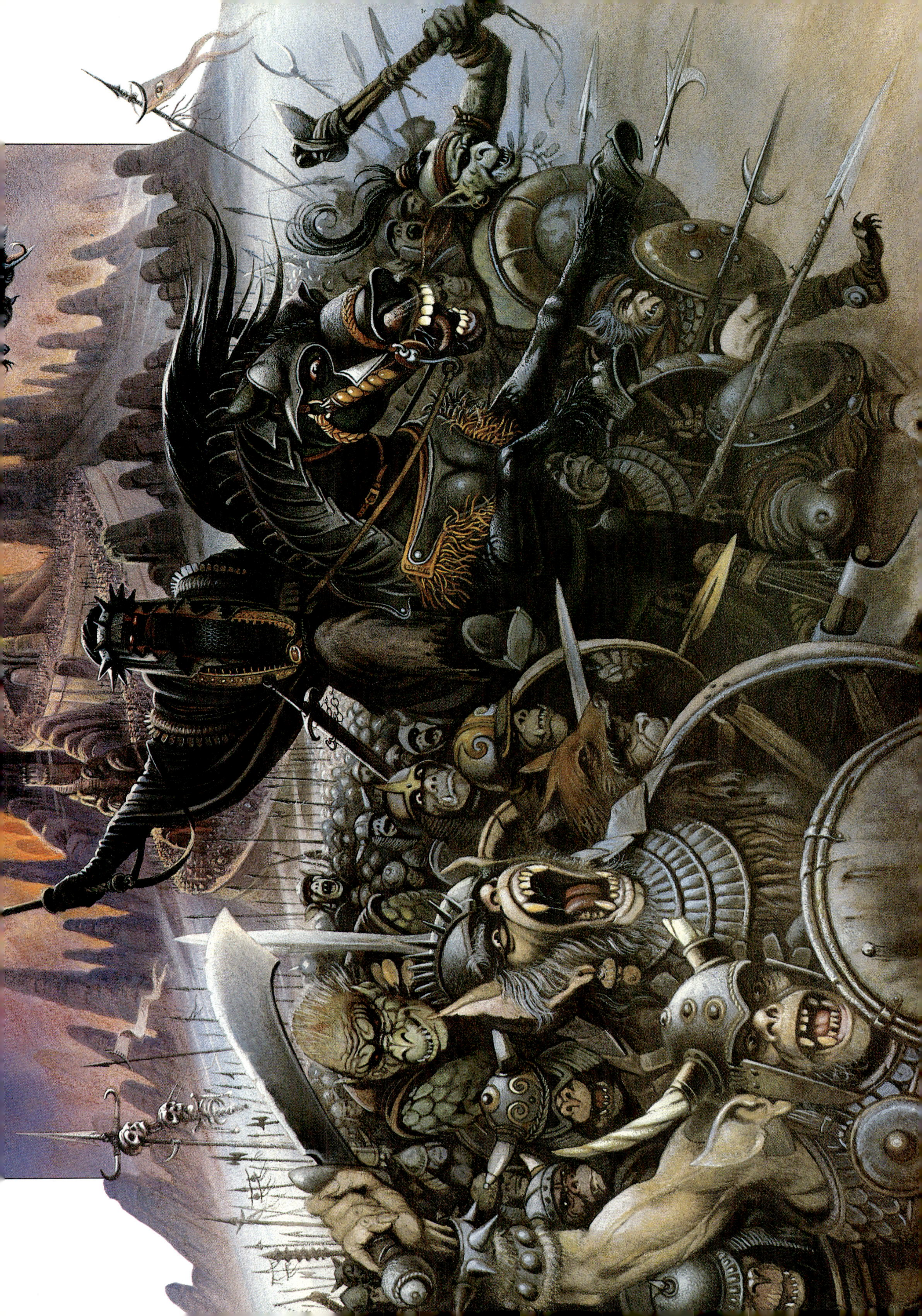

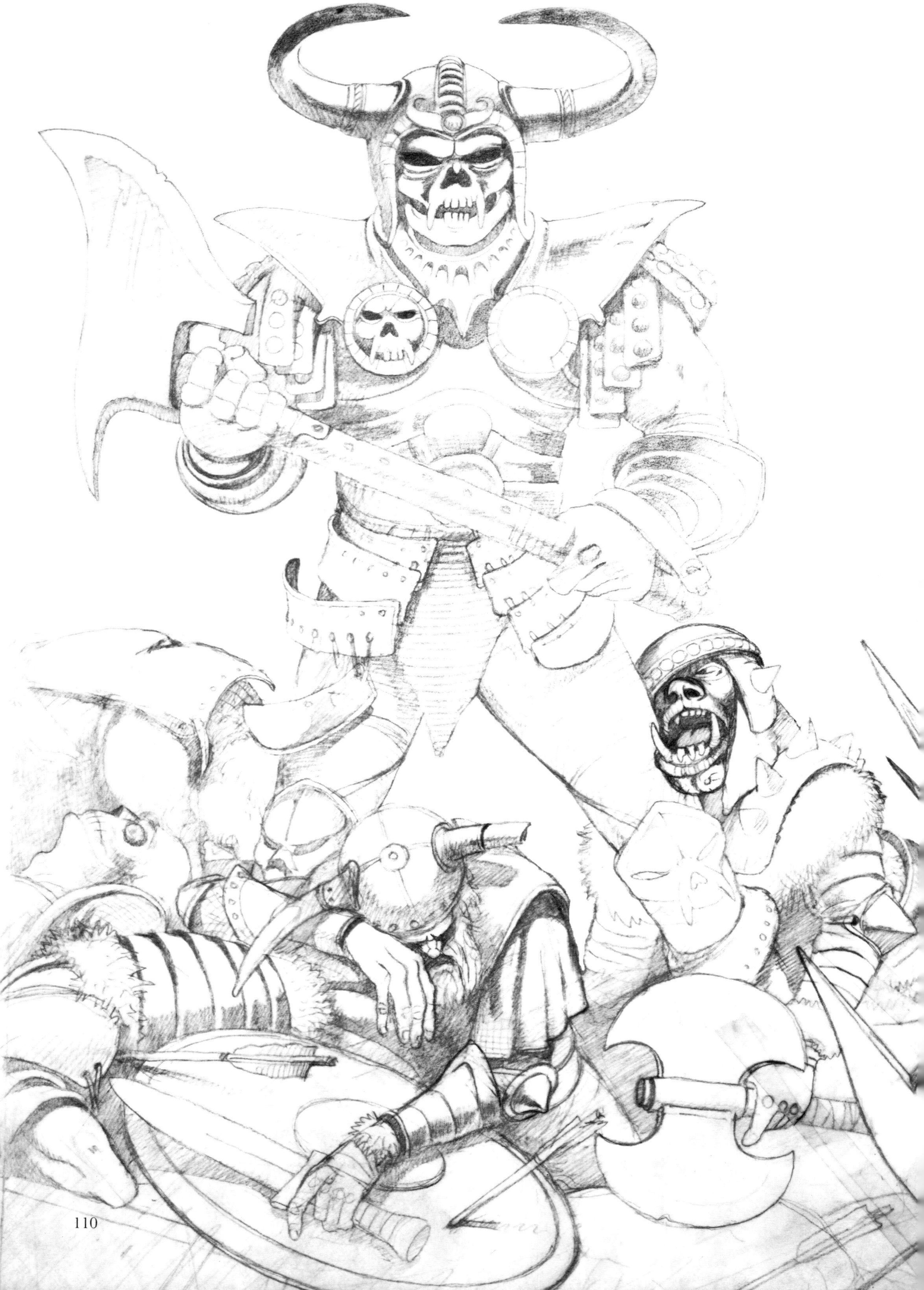

This commission was also for a game-box cover and was in fact the first picture I designed specifically for Fighting Fantasy. Before this, Games Workshop used pictures I had previously done for book covers.

The main figure was based on a tiny model that came with the game. A design point to notice is that everything in the picture points towards this figure, an effect strengthened in the finished painting by the background arch framing an insurgent army.

As with most Fighting Fantasy pictures it is a bit over the top, but that is what the genre is all about. The elements are drawn from Fantasy literature and myth, but restraint is thrown to the winds; anything goes.

My title, Who Dies First?, is taken from a Conan story in which he is at bay with an axe and daring his would-be assassins to approach.

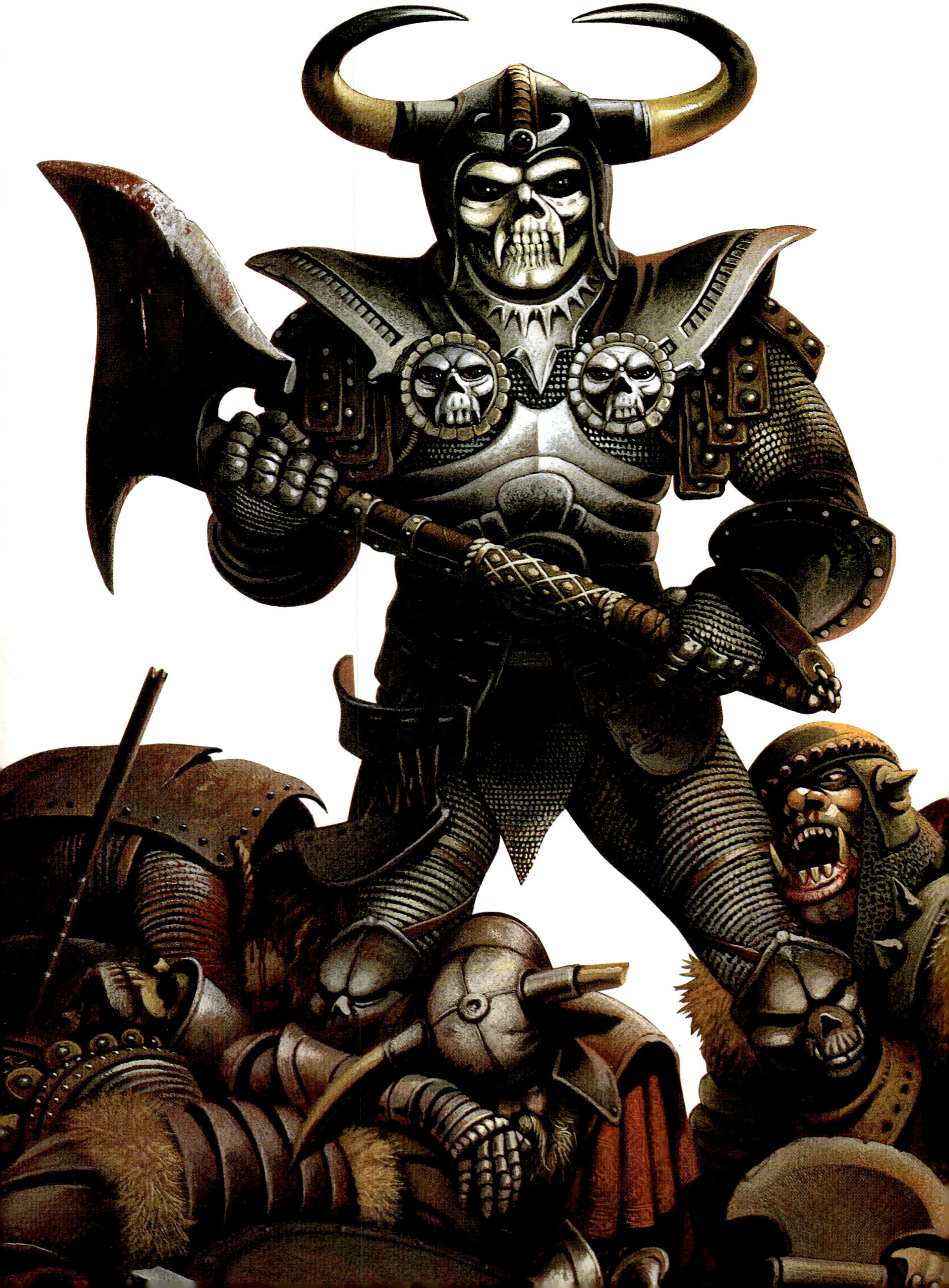

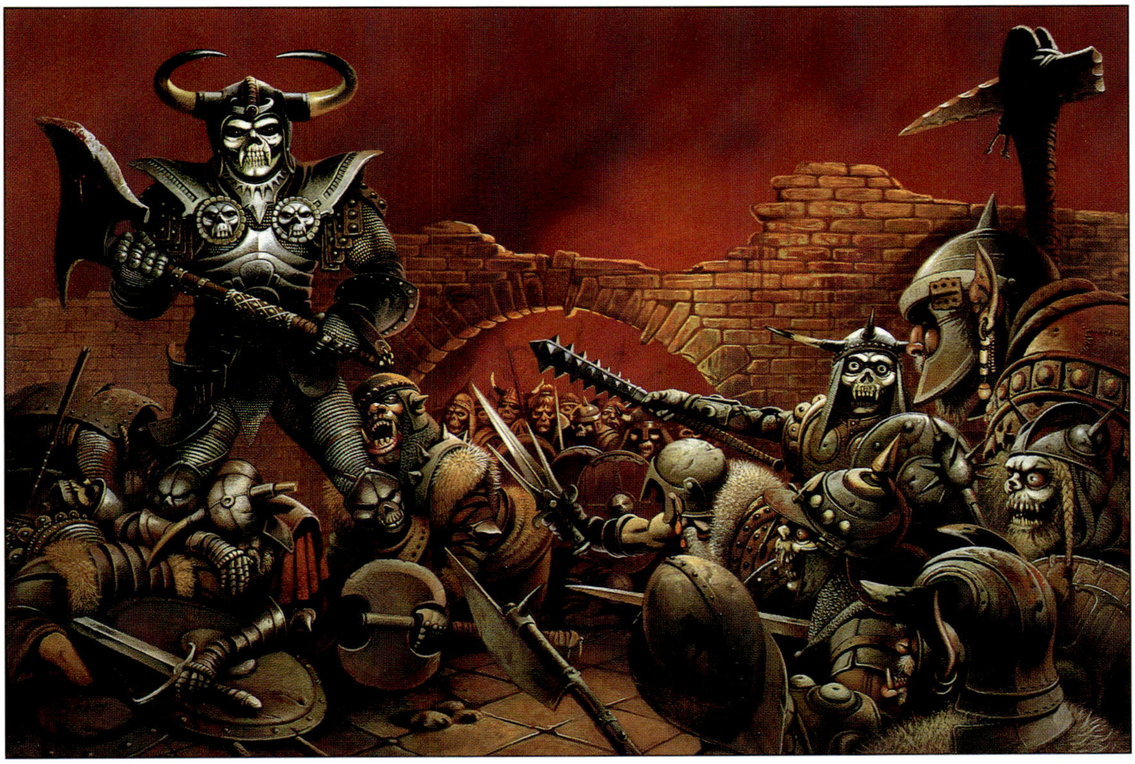

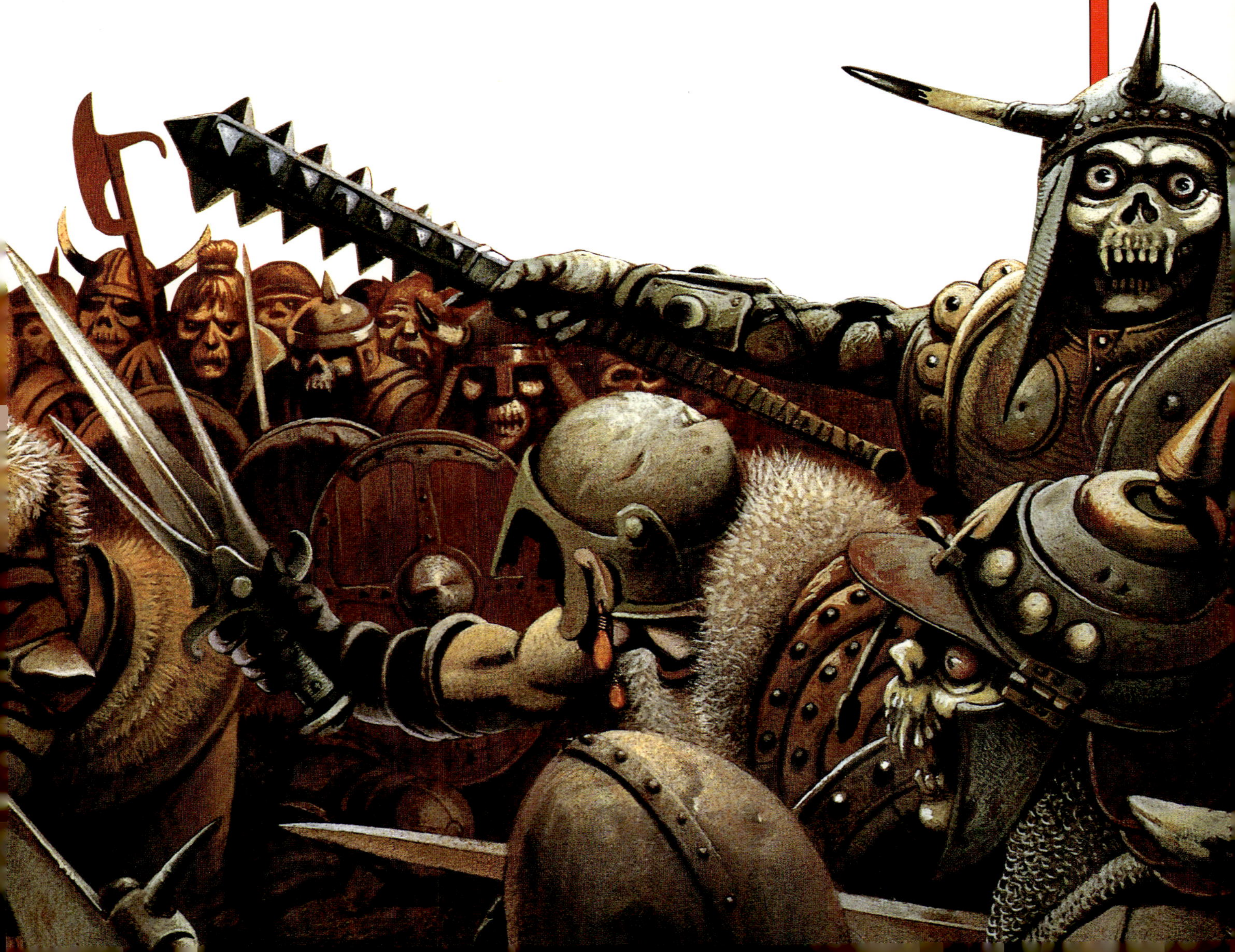

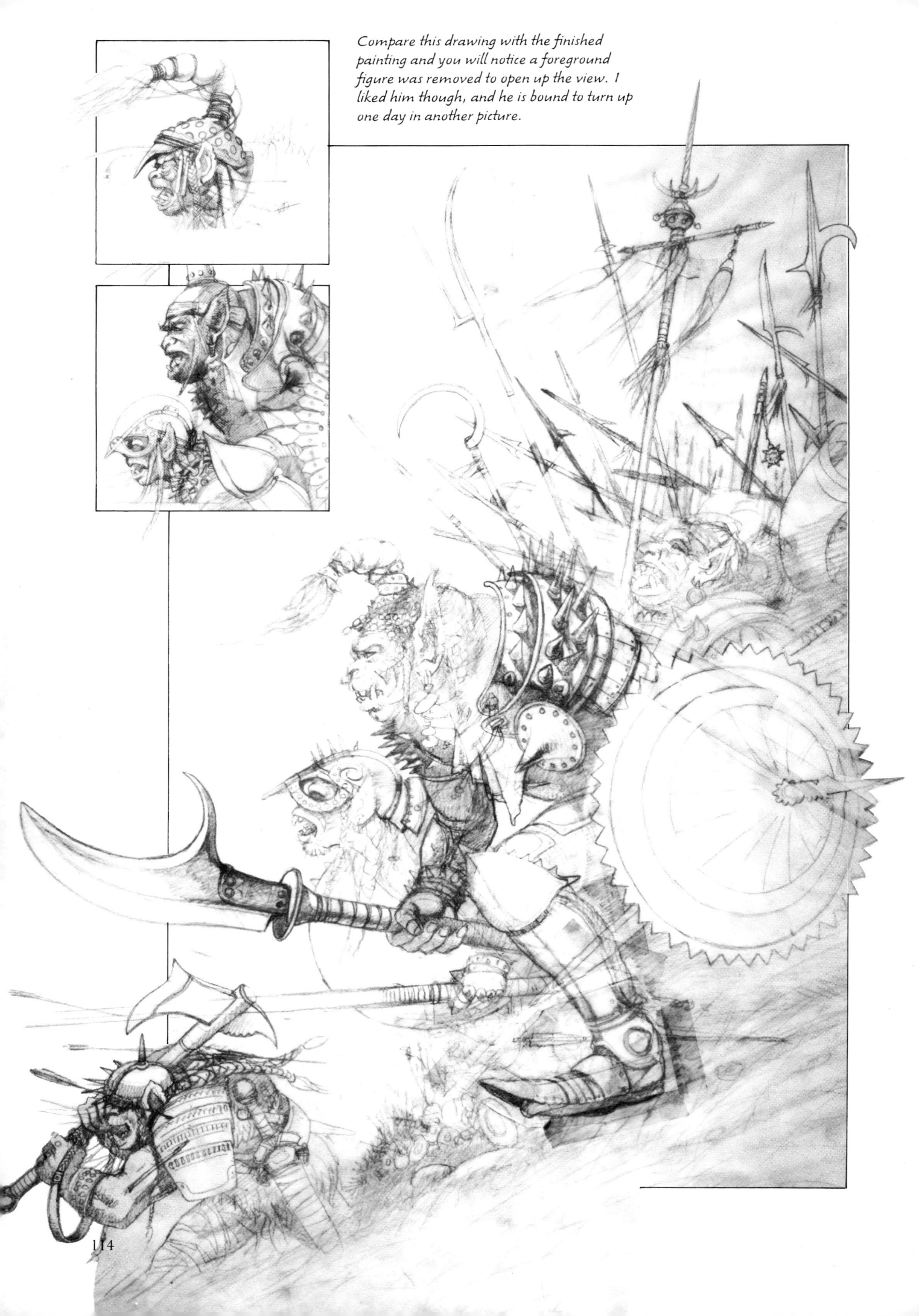

Compare this drawing with the finished painting and you will notice a foreground figure was removed to open up the view. I liked him though, and he is bound to turn up one day in another picture.

This was for a game-box cover. The concept was left to me, so I used an old sketch which could be adapted to the game's scenario. The medium is Chroma Colour on canvas board with touches of acrylic paint.

ORC CHARGE

116

BLOOD ROYAL

14 SKY WARRIORS

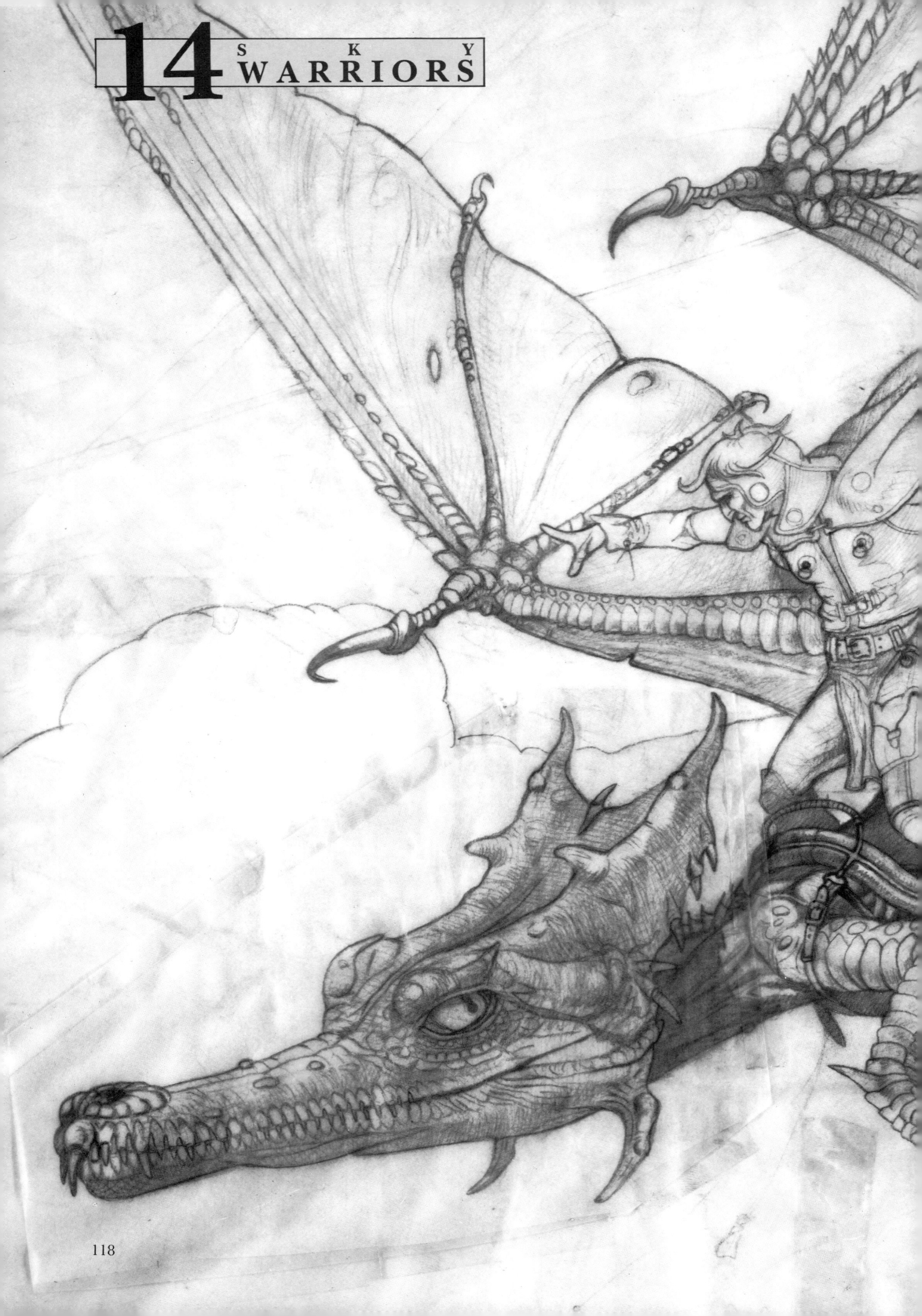

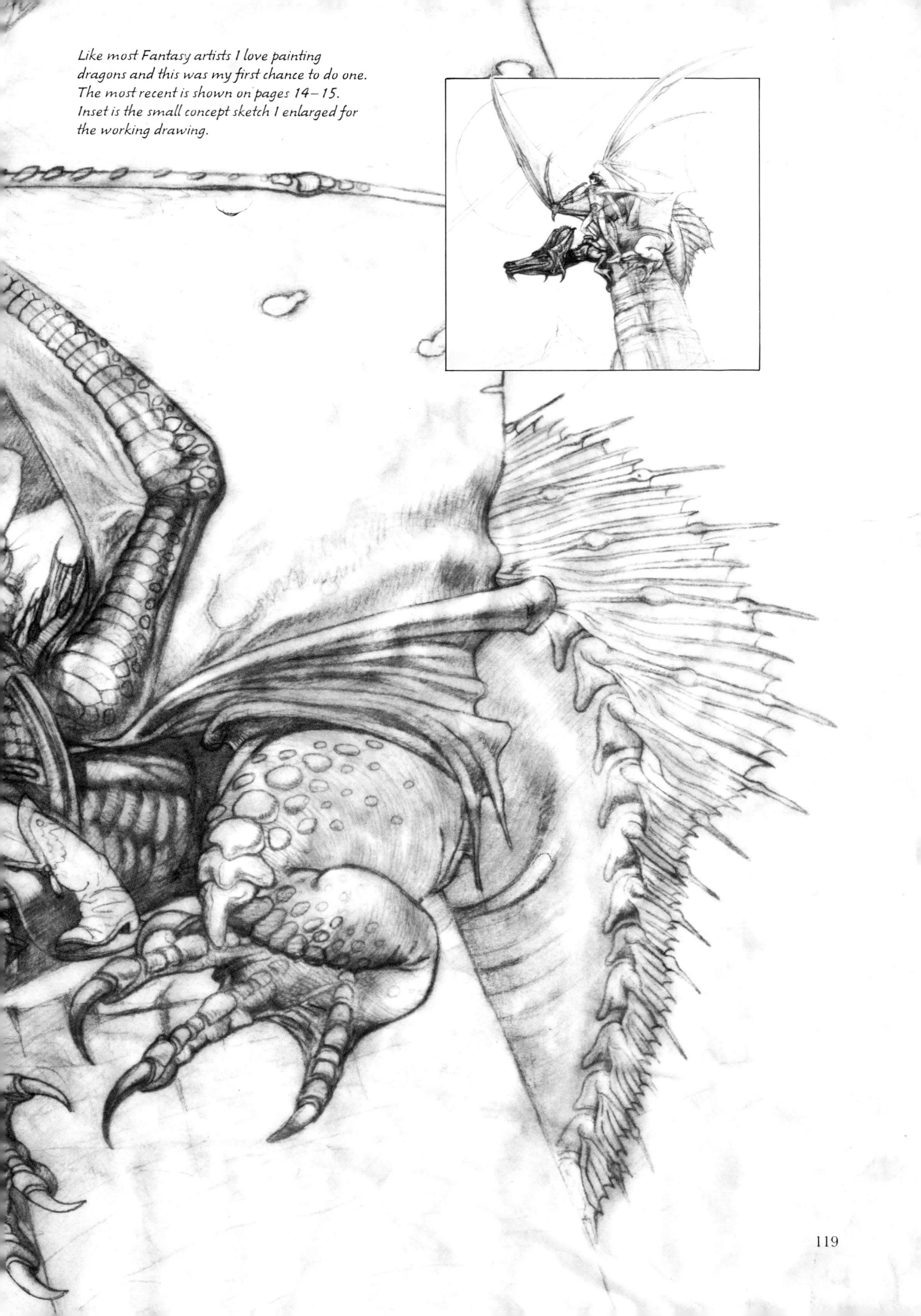

Like most Fantasy artists I love painting dragons and this was my first chance to do one. The most recent is shown on pages 14–15. Inset is the small concept sketch I enlarged for the working drawing.

The Nazgûl from The Lord of the Rings have been depicted many times before, but I relished the chance to do my own version of one. I based the flying creature on a prehistoric bird, so unlike a dragon it has no front claws. This is closer to nature anyway.

I wanted the rider to seem almost part of the bird and so blended their colours, but there was something missing until I introduced a contrasting red to the cloak lining.

A NAZGÛL

THE SENTINEL

121

Commissions like these give a chance to exercise my largely frustrated desire to design costumes for films. They were for a two-volume story and the publishers were so pleased they have been asking for similar covers ever since (see the example at the beginning on pages 6–7).

A pleasant change in book-cover fashion from the 1970s is that it is now possible to design more realistic and practical costumes without the publishers demanding more nudity. People usually think I'm the one who wants my heroines to bare all, even if they happen to be in the Arctic at the time, but it's not so.

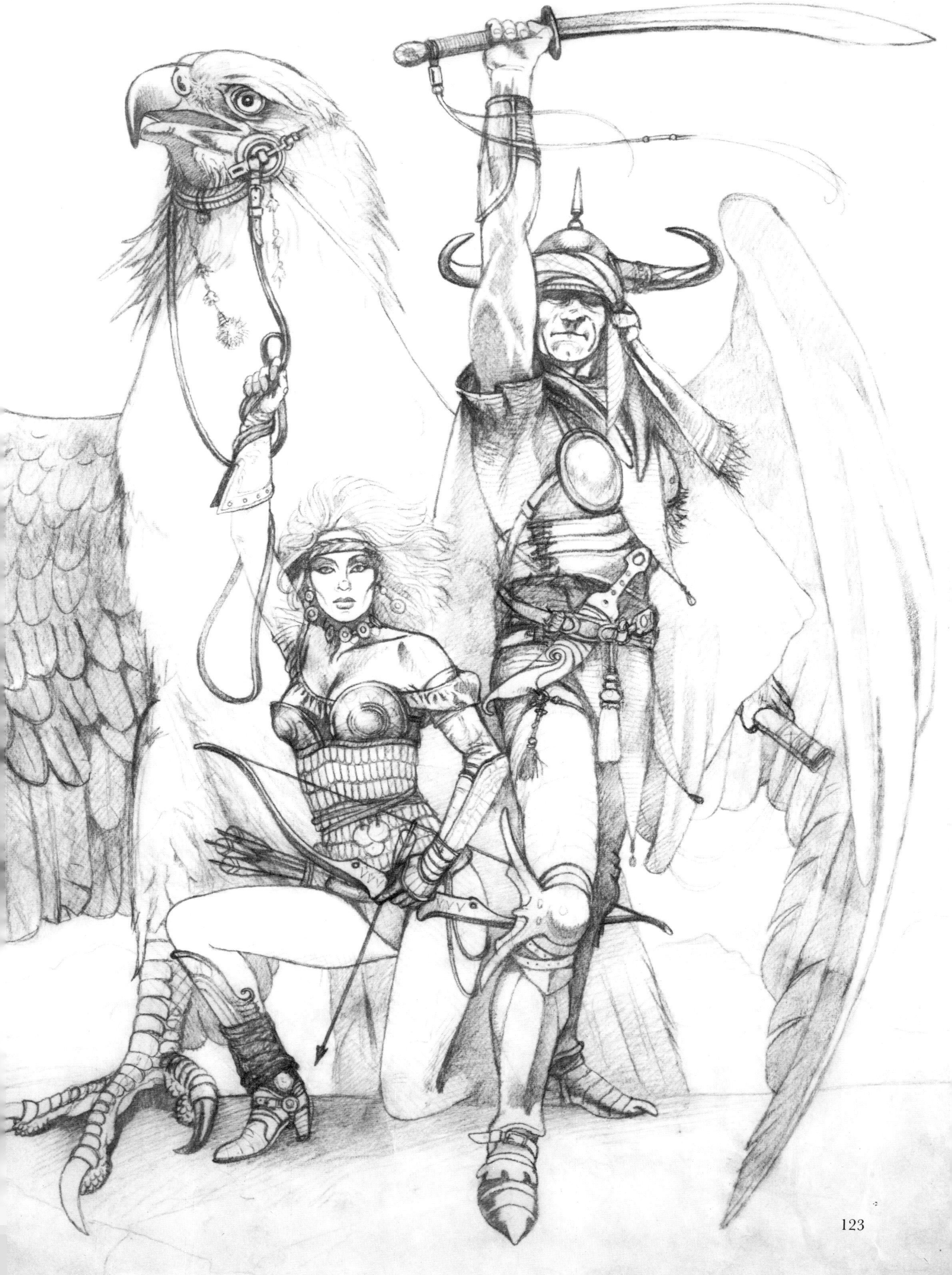

EAGLE RIDER

EAGLE WARRIORS

DEATH STRUGGLE

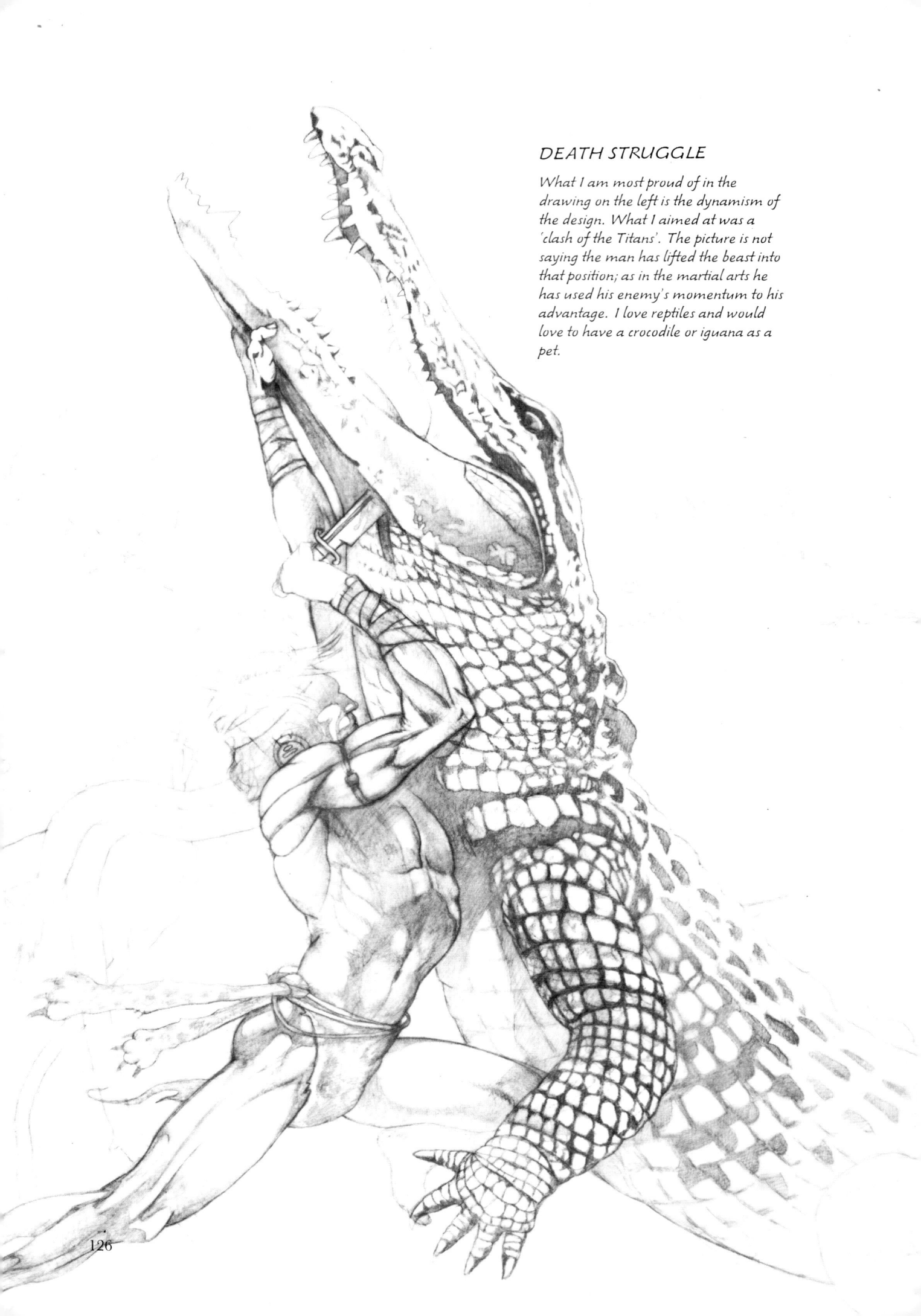

What I am most proud of in the drawing on the left is the dynamism of the design. What I aimed at was a 'clash of the Titans'. The picture is not saying the man has lifted the beast into that position; as in the martial arts he has used his enemy's momentum to his advantage. I love reptiles and would love to have a crocodile or iguana as a pet.

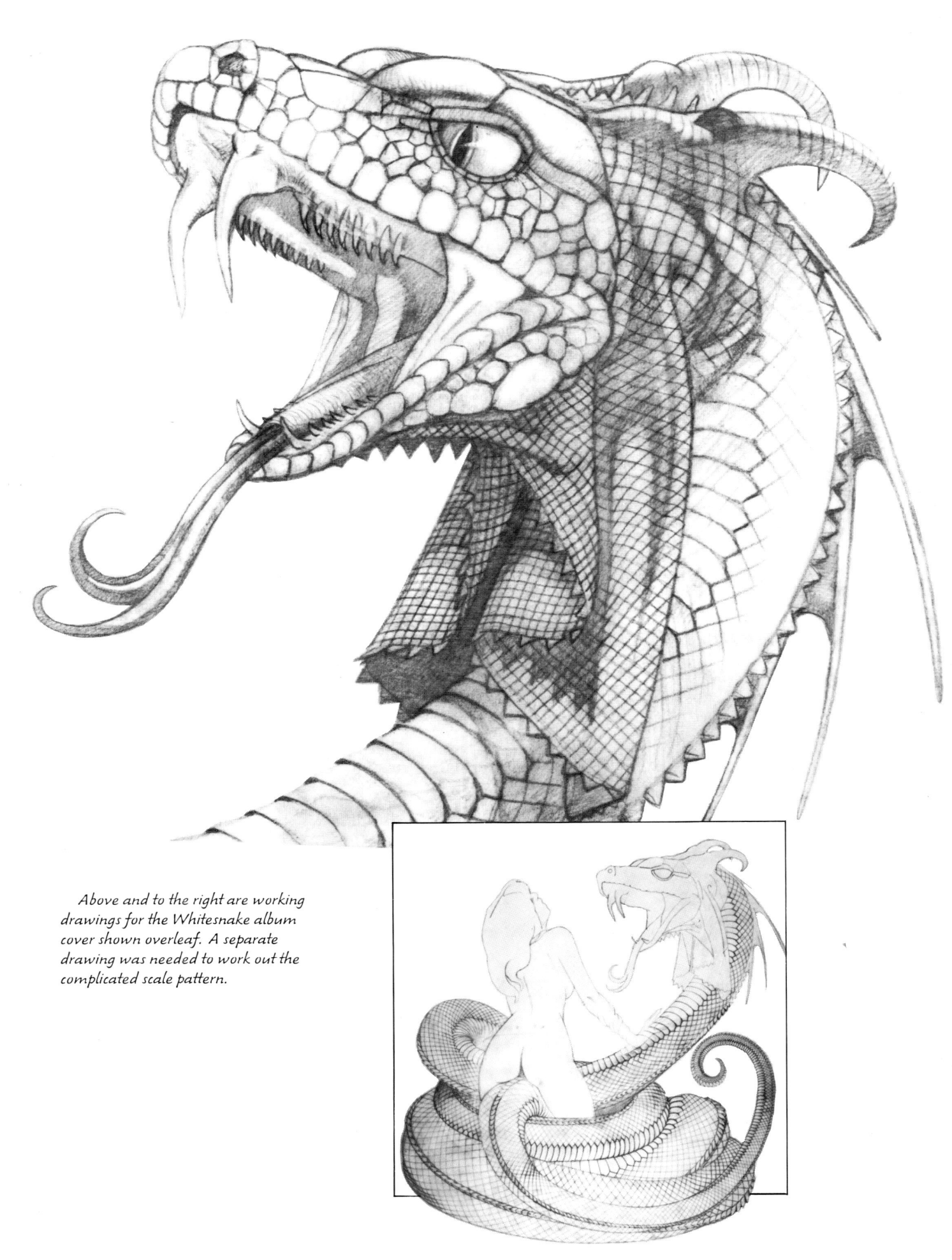

Above and to the right are working drawings for the Whitesnake album cover shown overleaf. A separate drawing was needed to work out the complicated scale pattern.

15 RECORD SLEEVES

In the 1970s there was a great surge in the popularity of Fantasy illustration for record covers, but Chris was not then in a position to take advantage of the trend. By the time he was, fashion had moved on leaving Heavy Metal bands as almost the only ones still interested in his kind of work.

Commissions have occasionally come his way, though, examples of which are shown here. The *Fallen Angel* sleeve, which opens out to show the full figure, was adapted from one of his *Raven* book covers, the other two were directly commissioned.

Fashion, perhaps prompted by feminist pressures, has also moved away from the portrayal of naked women on book and record covers. Chris's *Lovehunter* sleeve rather bucked the trend and has in fact earned him more abuse than almost any other picture. He is fairly unrepentant about it, although he does accept that using eroticism to sell things may be a kind of exploitation – up to a point. Perhaps, he says, pictures like this should be confined to men's magazines.

The *Krokus* cover was a recent commission. At the last moment Chris was asked to remove the winged figure, which he thinks a shame. He would like to do more of this kind of work and believes fashion will eventually come full circle to bring a fresh demand for illustrated record sleeves.

RAVEN

129

16 FILM AND VIDEOS

These concept drawings of posters for the film Hellraiser came about through my friendship with the writer Clive Barker, on whose story the film is based. I was invited along to the set and came up with these ideas, but in the end the American bosses decided to use a photographic poster.

THE LAMP

Here are some examples of a new line of work for Chris, covers for video films that lack any other promotional material for one reason or another, sometimes because they were originally B-films, sometimes because they were originally made for television. Usually Chris receives a copy of the video to view and from which to work out his concept, but occasionally he is simply sent a rough drawing.

The work is not quite as exciting as doing cinema posters and is complicated by Chris usually having to deal with a committee instead of a single art director, but he enjoys the involvement with the film world it provides, particularly since the general standard of such work is rising.

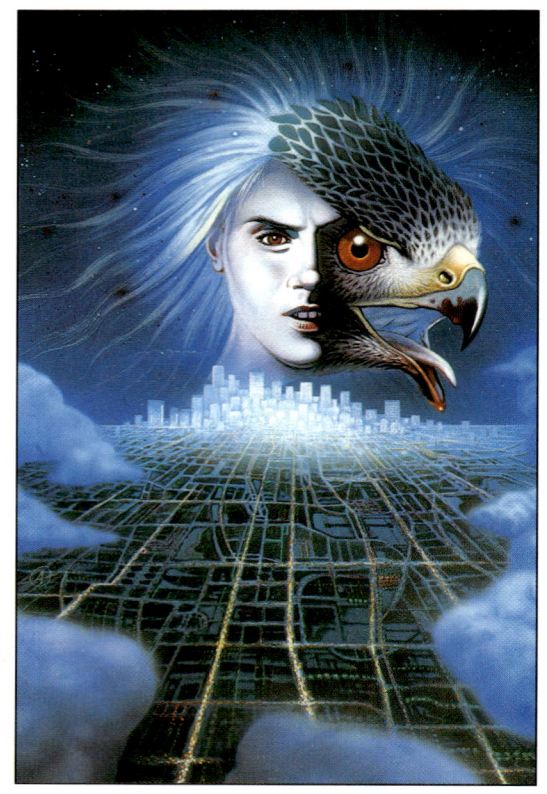

THE VISITOR

SWAMP THING

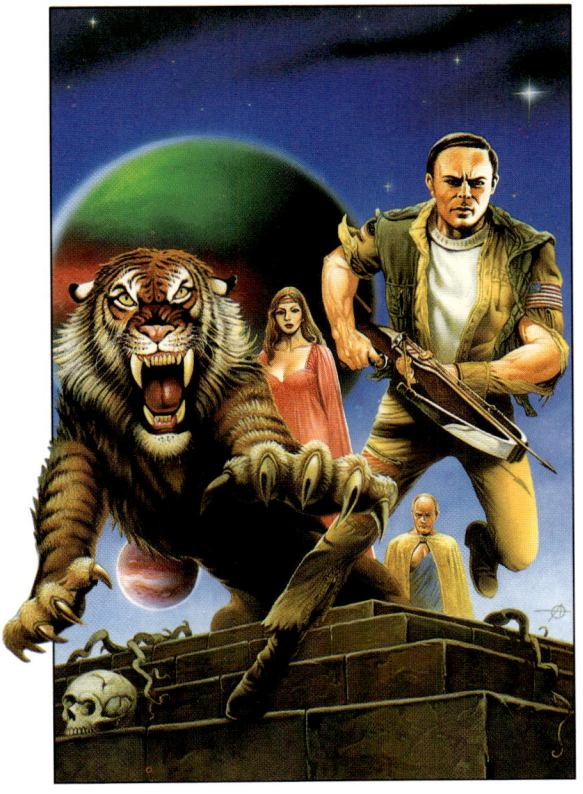

STRANGE NEW WORLD

CITY BENEATH THE SEA

133

STANDARD BEARER

This design was for one of a set of Raven books which gave me a great chance to combine my loves of Fantasy and painting pin-ups. The stories' heroine is terrific and I wish there were more like her that I could do covers for.

Shown here same size as original.

135

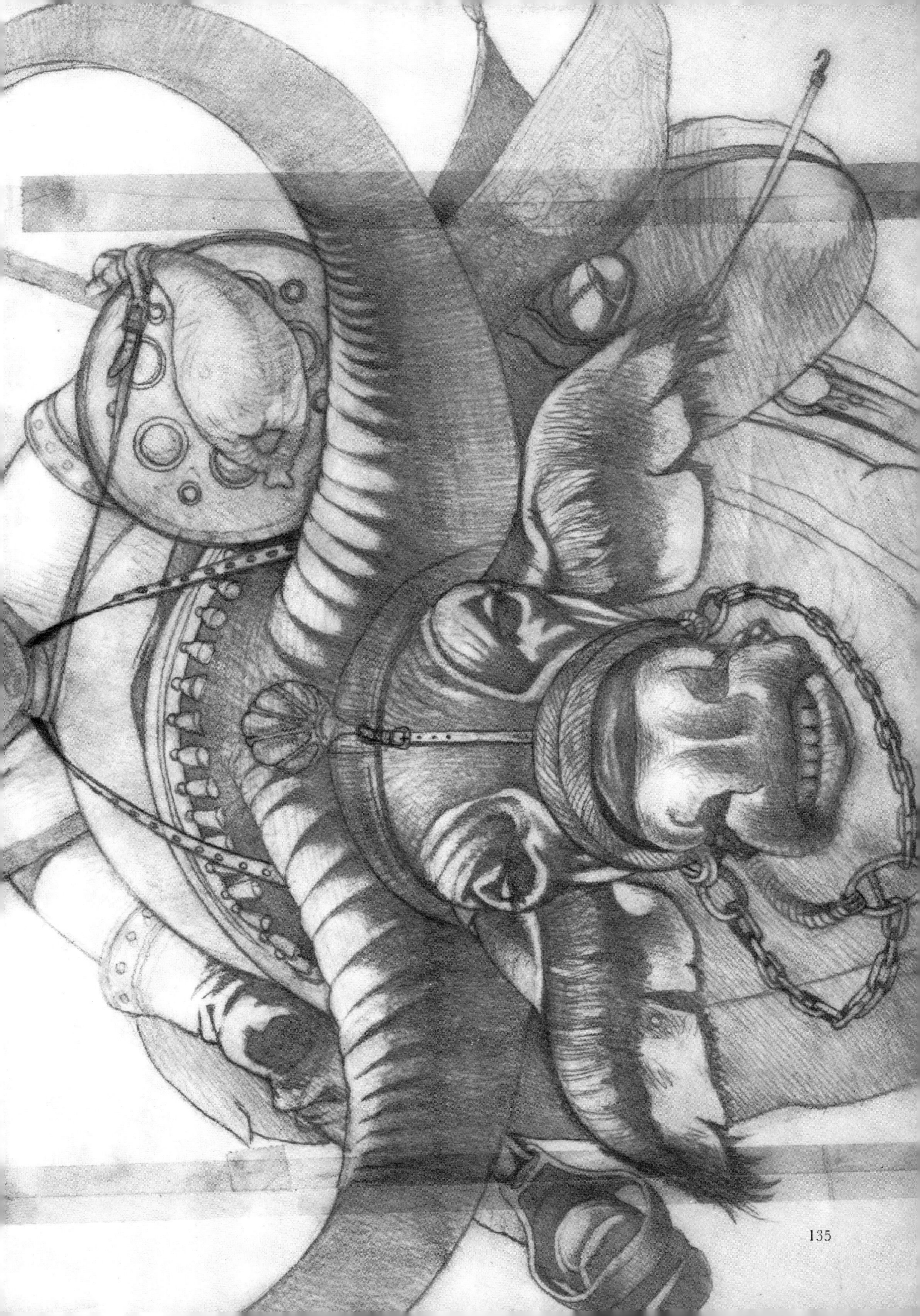

17 PIN-UPS

This picture was half a technical illustration exercise. The two main elements were worked out on separate sheets of tracing paper then brought together. My main problem was adapting the girl's pose to fit the camera exactly.

I decided on a very simple scheme with basically only three colours – grey, mauve and flesh-tone. Choosing a grey background took some courage because the camera still had to stand out against it, but I solved the problem by graduating the tone, having it dark at the top to contrast with the flash unit and pale at the bottom to contrast with the camera body.

WATCH THE BIRDY

In the final painting of this beach scene I left out the background wreckage because it distracted the eye from the main figure and it was obvious enough anyway that she has been washed up from a wreck.

The small portrait on the left was done for a women's magazine a long time ago. It is mostly a pencil drawing with some airbrushing of very gentle tones.

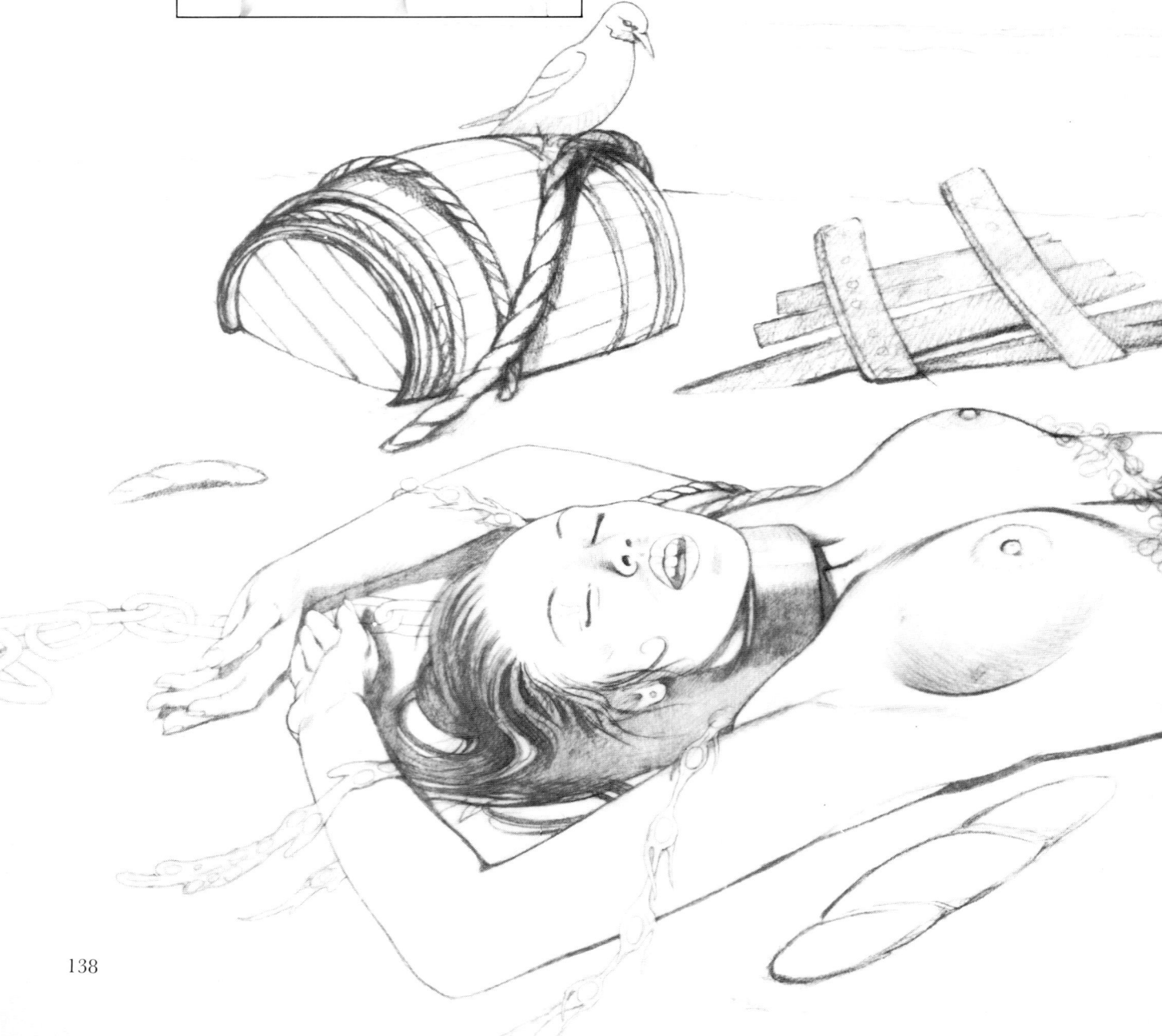

STRANGER ON THE SHORE

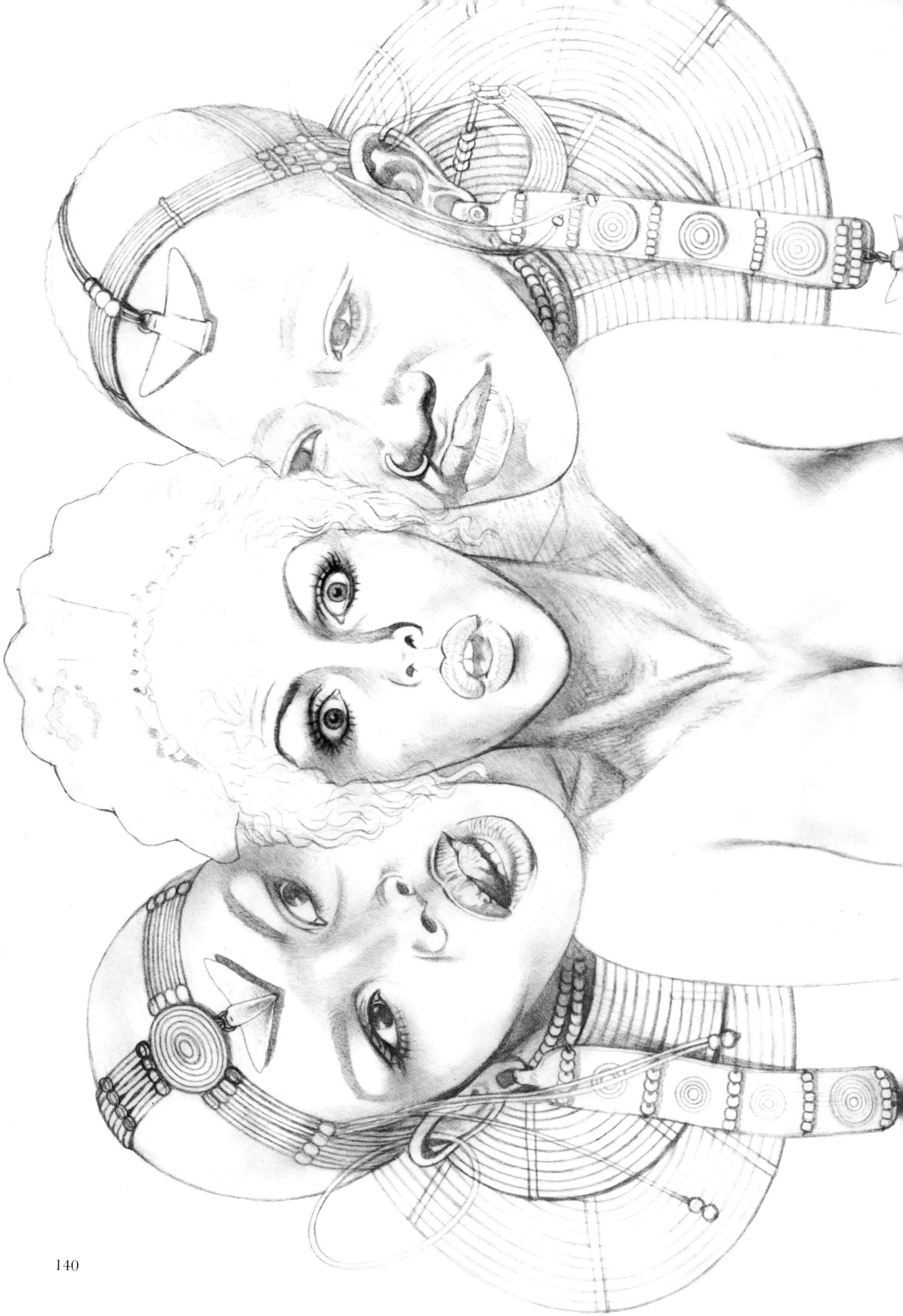

LIGHT AND SHADE

People often imagine that I just sit down with a piece of illustration board and work away until a finished painting emerges, but my technique usually leaves me with at least one large, very detailed drawing for every finished painting.

With a simple composition like this which can be done all in one, the working drawing ends up almost as a black and white version of the painting.

AFTERWORD

EROTIC MEMOIRS

Finally, a note on this book's title. Chris chose it mainly because it gave a chance to fulfil an old ambition of painting Medusa, who is the opposite of the usual conception, i.e. terrifyingly beautiful instead of terrifyingly ugly.

There is some support for this in the Greek legends. Most agree that Medusa was originally very beautiful and had her abundant hair turned into snakes for daring to vie with the goddess Athene. Many also say that Athene guided Perseus' hand when he slew Medusa, or at least blessed his venture, so she may still have had cause for jealousy.

The effect Chris aimed for in his painting was almost that of a sculpture coming to life. At the back of his mind was the ancient Greek custom of painting their statues vividly so that they looked very lifelike and different to how we see them today. So the snakes have a metallic sheen and Medusa's skin is like ivory. Only the eyes and lips are fully alive.

INDEX

p.1	MEDUSA title lettering & drawing, 1987.
pp.4–5	JUNGLE GIRL drawing, 1979.
pp.6–7	
pp.8–9	THE QUEST drawing, 1982.
pp.14–15	DRAGONSPELL book cover. Penguin Books Ltd.
pp.16–19	Early work.
pp.20–21	Tattoos.
pp.22–29	SPARTACUS drawings and paintings for Jeff Wayne's musical project.
pp.30–37	HEROIC DREAM drawings and stages to finished book cover. Paper Tiger.
pp.38–45	JUDGE ANDERSON drawings and stages to finished book cover. Games Workshop Ltd.
pp.46–53	THE SIRENS' REMORSE drawings and stages to finished book cover. Paper Tiger.
pp.54–61	THE ORC'S WAR BANNER drawings and stages to finished book cover. Puffin Books Ltd.
pp.62–65	Graphic work commissioned by Visnews facilities, New Opportunity Press, Granada Books and Tandem Books.
pp.66–75	HEAVY METAL studies and final poster for the film, 1980. Columbia Pictures.
pp.76–81	STARTREK book covers and working drawings, 1983–4. Corgi Books Ltd.
pp.82–84	THE PROTECTOR drawings and film poster detail. Warner Bros 1985.
p.85	MARINE ISSUE film poster, video cover. Warner Bros.
pp.86–89	SUPERGIRL drawings and finished posters. Warner Bros 1984.
p.96	MAASAI portfolio illustration 1979. Paper Tiger.

	CHEYENNE model by Fine Art Castings Ltd.	p.124	EAGLE RIDER book cover. New English Library, 1984.
p.97	CHEYENNE calendar illustration 1983. Iguana Pub. Ltd.	p.125	EAGLE WARRIORS book cover. New English Library, 1983.
pp.100–101	HAREM GUARD magazine illustration. *Men Only*. 1980.	p.126	DEATH STRUGGLE drawing, 1978.
	JUNGLE GIRL magazine portfolio illustration. Paper Tiger Books 1979.	p.128	KROKUS record cover. M.C.A. Records Inc. 1988.
	THE PARTISAN spec. design, 1982.	p.129	FALLEN ANGEL record cover. Bronze Records Ltd, 1978.
pp.104–105	MISS AMERICA magazine illustration. *Men Only*. 1979.		LOVEHUNTER record cover. Sunburst Records Ltd, 1979.
	STARSHIP CAPTAIN calendar illustration. Iguana Pub. 1981.	pp.130–1	HELLRAISER concept drawings for film poster. New World Pictures.
	MODEL 2000 spec. design 1985.	pp.132–3	Video covers. Warner Bros Home Videos.
pp.108–109	THE HOST OF MORDOR game box cover. Games Workshop Ltd, 1984.		THE LAMP. Medusa Communications Ltd.
pp.112–113	WHO DIES FIRST? game box cover. Games Workshop Ltd, 1984.	pp.134–5	STANDARD BEARER drawing, 1978.
p.116	ORC CHARGE book illustration. Puffin Books, 1985.	p.137	WATCH THE BIRDY magazine illustration. *Men Only*, 1982.
p.117	BLOOD ROYAL game box cover. Games Workshop Ltd.	pp.138–9	STRANGER ON THE SHORE drawing, 1982.
p.120	NAZGÛL magazine cover. Computer and Video Games, 1985.	p.141	LIGHT AND SHADE magazine illustration. *Men Only*, 1983.
p.121	THE SENTINEL book cover. Sphere Books, 1979.	pp.142–3	EROTIC MEMOIRS drawing, 1982.

ACKNOWLEDGEMENTS

I would like to thank all those people who commissioned the illustrations that appear in this book. I would also especially like to thank Patrick Woodroffe, Nigel Suckling, Ian Huebner, Hubert Schaafsma and Graham Bush, since without their help this book would never have been produced.